DISCARD

Too late!

The woman who'd dropped out of the trees behind him had the slim, deadly rifle in her hands pointed at his navel. Derrick stared, startled by her sudden appearance and angry at himself for being startled. Mistakes got men killed. He couldn't afford to make them.

"Who are you?" she demanded. "And what do you want?" Her rifle never wavered from its deadly aim.

She was tall but lean, fine-boned and elegant, with the kind of body that should have been sheathed in curve-clinging silk. Instead she wore a rumpled khaki shirt and walking shorts. Her silken brown hair, almost black, was drawn back in a ponytail that kept it off her neck. Her nose was a tad too long for her finely sculpted face, her mouth a little too wide. *Too wide, yet eminently kissable…*

"I'm looking for E. B. Bradshaw," he said. "That's you, right?"

Dear Reader,

Rain forests fascinate me. I've visited the rain forests of
the Upper Amazon and the Orinoco, and I live in an island
rain forest now. With orchids, I might add. Lots and lots of
orchids. Flamboyant masses and shy little gems that are all
too easy to miss. Orchids in trees, orchids in pots, orchids in
the garden and orchids, always, in the house.

The orchids aren't the only attraction, of course. A rain
forest is an amazing place to live, though it does take awhile
to get used to all the critters that come with it: spiders and
centipedes longer than my spread hand, termites and giant
cockroaches, ants and mosquitoes and rats and…well,
you get the picture! Paradise has always come with a few
unpleasant secrets lurking in the undergrowth. That's one
price you pay for living there.

More than the rain forests themselves, however, I have
always been fascinated by the tales of the people who have
journeyed, often alone, into the jungles' darkest depths.
They go in search of treasure, orchids or adventure, gold or
timber or lost civilizations, perhaps. But the lucky ones, it
seems to me, aren't the ones who find the treasure they went
to seek, but the ones who, often in the midst of the greatest
danger, manage to unlock at least some of the secrets hidden
deep in their all-too-human hearts.

This story is about two of the lucky ones.

Anne

OPERATION: RESCUE

Anne Woodard

Silhouette®
Romantic
SUSPENSE

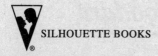 SILHOUETTE BOOKS

ISBN-13: 978-0-373-27576-2
ISBN-10:   0-373-27576-5

OPERATION: RESCUE

Books by Anne Woodard

Silhouette Romantic Suspense

Dead Aim #1296
Operation: Rescue #1506

Other books written under the name Anne Avery

Harlequin Historical

The Lawman Takes a Wife #573
The Bride's Revenge #618

ANNE WOODARD

After much wandering, Anne Woodard recently put down
roots in Hawaii. With writing, cutting back a garden that
won't stop growing and breaking up doggie squabbles
because the Todd Man stole everyone's bones, she keeps
busy. But not so busy that she can't explore the beauties of
her new home state, including the local beaches! Readers
can contact Anne at annewoodard1@earthlink.net.

To my aunt Laura Levi, with thanks for her interest and
support through all these years.

Chapter 1

The jungle heat was like a living thing, voracious and malign, sucking the life out of him, drop by precious drop. The black steel of the AK-47 was slick under his grip, damp with the moisture that hung in the air and made every breath he took an effort.

He had trained in the jungle, lived in it, made love in it. Hunted in it for the two-legged killers that hid in its green depths. But it was the last place in the world he'd want to die.

It was the last place Danny would want to die.

Derrick brushed back a heavy vine trailing across the path, then swore as a slim green snake tumbled onto the ground at his feet, twisted over the toe of his boot, righted itself and slithered out of sight. He couldn't tell if it was one of the half dozen or so types of poisonous snakes to be found in this damned jungle, and he didn't care. Snake bites were the least of his worries....

Everyone who knew the situation on the island had

agreed: if he was going to get his brother out of this jungle alive, there was only one person he could absolutely trust to get him where he had to go as fast as he had to get there—Bradshaw.

Orchid hunter, botanist, research scientist, *Dr.* E. B. Bradshaw had grown up on Pilenau and was as at home in the jungle as the indigenous tribes that still lived in its depths and hunted their prey with poison-tipped darts. For a fee—a very hefty fee, he'd been told—Bradshaw had guided others into the jungle and brought out a few lost adventurers everyone believed could never be found.

Whatever the fee, Derrick didn't care. If Bradshaw could get him through this hell of a jungle ahead of the Pilenau army, he'd mortgage his soul if he had to.

In country like this, where the best satellite images in the world could give you a leaf-by-leaf view of the dense jungle canopy but only occasional glimpses of the treacherous jungle floor a hundred or more feet below, a skilled guide could mean the difference between mission success and mission failure.

And when failure meant that Danny might die, Derrick would grab at every advantage he could get. Grab, hell! For the sake of the younger brother he'd failed so often, Derrick would flat out *take* what he needed. And what he needed now was an experienced guide.

The fact that Bradshaw was a woman didn't matter….

Bradshaw's camp was right where it was supposed to be. Bradshaw was nowhere in sight.

Derrick stood in the middle of the clearing, rifle at

the ready, warily eyeing his surroundings. It wasn't much of a camp, just a small cleared area with two well-worn tents set on crude wooden platforms a couple feet off the ground. The tent on the right was small, large enough for two if they were really, really friendly. The flaps on the tent were down, no doubt hiding a cot and maybe a box of clothes and personal possessions. It wouldn't be much, and judging by the rest of the place, it definitely wouldn't be valuable.

The sides on the larger tent were rolled up, exposing the rough wooden planking that served as the floor, a crude worktable, a few heavy-duty plastic chests that probably protected papers and research materials, a chair and smaller table half-buried under untidy stacks of books, and a makeshift kitchen—rough-sawn planks laid over crates turned on their sides in lieu of cabinets. The crates were filled with cookware, dishes, canned food and plastic tubs sealed tight against the insects that otherwise would have devoured the rice and sugar and other staples they probably contained.

He'd wondered why someone living alone in the jungle hadn't worried about leaving a camp unattended for days at a time. Especially in a place like Pilenau, where anything of value that wasn't tied down or locked up tended to grow legs and walk away. Now he knew. There wasn't a hell of a lot to steal, and, this deep in the jungle, what there was probably wasn't worth the effort of hauling away.

The place looked empty, but the coffeepot on the small camp stove steamed gently, the scientific papers and hand-written notes laid out on the makeshift work-table arranged as if someone had been working on them only a few moments before.

Slowly, he pivoted on one foot, scanning the camp, the jungle, the trail he'd just covered. Bradshaw was here. But…where?

A soft rustle of leaves and a softer thump at his back made him spin around, rifle at the ready. Too late. The woman who'd dropped out of the trees behind him had the slim, deadly rifle in her hands pointed at his navel. Even from ten feet away he could see that the safety was off and that she held it like a person who slept with the damned thing and liked it.

Derrick stared, startled by her sudden appearance and angry at himself for being startled. Mistakes got men killed. He couldn't afford to make them.

The woman in front of him clearly wouldn't be inclined to let him make another.

He studied her appreciatively.

She was tall, almost as tall as his own six feet, but lean, fine-boned and elegant. She had the kind of body that should have been sheathed in curve-clinging silk. Instead, she wore a rumpled khaki shirt and walking shorts that looked like they'd been washed on a rock.

Her hair, a silken brown that was almost black, was drawn back in a practical and unbecoming ponytail that kept it off her neck. Her nose was a tad too long for her finely sculpted face, her mouth a little too wide. Too wide, yet eminently kissable…

Her assessing gaze swept past him to study his back trail, then swung back to pin him in his place.

"Who are you?" she demanded. "And what do you want?" Her rifle never wavered from its deadly aim on his gut.

Derrick lifted his hands from his own rifle and held them up, palms out.

"I'm looking for E. B. Bradshaw, the orchid hunter," he said. "That's you, right?"

Again that disconcerting, unblinking gaze.

"I am she," she said at last, the clipped, precisely grammatical words as sharp as the *parang,* the local version of a machete, dangling from a loop at her waist. "And you still haven't answered my questions."

"My name's Marx," he said. "Derrick Marx."

"And you're here because…?" She pointedly left the question dangling.

"I need a guide and I'm told you're the best person for the job."

"A guide to where? And for what?"

She didn't waste words. He liked that. It made explaining things a hell of a lot simpler.

"My brother is being held hostage by the Sword of God. I intend to get him out."

For the first time, the muzzle of her rifle wavered. "The Sword of God? They *kill* people. Or hadn't you heard?"

"I'd heard. That's why I need your help."

"To do what? Get you both killed?"

"I need you to get me to their camp, as quickly as possible."

"Ah. My mistake. You want to get all *three* of us killed." She couldn't quite pull off the sneer.

"Could we sit down while we talk about it?" He cocked his head in the direction of the larger tent but took care not to let his hands drop anywhere near his rifle. "I wouldn't say no to a cup of that coffee if you offered."

If he could get her talking, he just might convince her to help him. If he had to share a few facts he'd prefer to keep to himself, then so be it. Whatever it took.

And if the truth didn't convince her, he and Bear had worked out a damned good lie that would.

For a second, he wasn't sure she'd bite. He might as well try to read a rock as her expressionless face. Just when he decided she'd refuse, she slowly lowered her rifle. Derrick stifled his automatic sigh of relief.

"Slide your rifle off, slow and easy, and set it down there against that tree." She gestured with her rifle. "Drop your pack beside it."

Since she hadn't taken her finger off the trigger, Derrick did what she said, then stepped away, hands still high.

"Cups are in that box over there with the rest of the dishware." Her voice was deep for a woman, sexy and a little rough around the edges, as if she didn't use it much. "Sugar's in that plastic container on the table. No cream. No canned milk."

He cautiously lowered his hands. "Black's fine."

Was it his imagination, or had one corner of her mouth twitched in amusement?

Derrick picked a mug at random, used the frayed tea

towel hanging on a hook as a hot pad on the enameled
tin pot, and poured out a half cup of the blackest coffee
he'd ever seen. He took a brash swig. The hot, inky
brew was all the way to the back of his mouth before
his taste buds rebelled. His throat seized. His eyes
teared. It was all he could do to choke it down instead
of spit it out.

"What the hell *is* that stuff?" he spluttered, holding
the mug away from him in distaste.

She laughed. It was an intriguingly sexy laugh, even
if it was at his expense.

"It's the local coffee. Or what passes for coffee,
anyway. God knows what they put in it. I've never had
the courage to ask." She slid her finger off the trigger.
He could see the tension in her shoulders ease. "There's
a spoon by the sugar. Three heaping spoonfuls will just
about make that drinkable."

He poured in three, gingerly sipped, then added a
fourth before claiming the worn camp chair she'd indicated. The chair's battered wood frame creaked under
his weight. The canvas back and seat sagged. It wasn't
the kind of chair you got out of easily.

Derrick settled deeper into the chair, then took
another cautious sip of the coffee. Four sugars helped.
"What do they use this stuff for? Snake bite?"

"Only if you live long enough." The amusement was
gone.

She hesitated, then slipped her rifle's sling over her
head, set the weapon against the far side of the small
table in front of him and casually propped her hip

against the table's edge. The *parang* at her side clunked against the chipped wood. She didn't seem to notice.

Derrick couldn't help but admire her strategy. His rifle was twenty feet away. Hers was right at her fingertips and out of his reach. She was on her feet, able to react instantly to any threat. He was in a sagging canvas chair with a corner of the table dividing him from her. If he tipped the table over as a distraction, the books, canned foods and kitchen miscellany piled atop it would scatter across the tent's floor, as much a hazard to him as to her. If he tried to take her, she'd have her rifle pointed squarely between his eyes before he ever got to his feet.

She shouldn't have pinned the *parang* against the table, though.

As proof he was no threat, he stretched out his legs, crossed them at the ankle and smiled up at her, enjoying the view. There was a lot more to admire about E. B. Bradshaw than just her strategic sense.

Was it his imagination, or was that a blush rising under her tan?

"If the coffee's this strong, what's the local moonshine like?"

"Trust me. You don't want to know." She shoved away from the table abruptly, as if suddenly needing a little more distance between them.

"What branch of the military are you?" She wasn't looking at him, but the too-fast pulse visible at the base of her throat betrayed her. She was as intensely aware of him as he was of her.

"I used to be Special Forces."

"And now?"

"I'm a senior consultant with Hudson Security International. We advise corporations on how to keep their facilities and their personnel safe. We also provide bodyguards and security details if the company wants. And are willing to pay for it," he added dryly.

Her gaze swung up to meet his. "Even in war zones?"

"*Especially* in war zones."

"So why not use those resources? Why come to me?"

"Because you're here and they're not. Yet. Because you know the area and they don't. And because I don't want to risk alerting the Sword by flying surveillance in a chopper. By the time I've got Danny out of that camp, friends from Hudson will be here to evacuate him. In the meantime…"

In the meantime, a lot could go very, very wrong.

He shrugged, forcing away the thought. "In the meantime, I hoof it. And you're the person best qualified to show me the way."

Without alerting the Sword *or* the army.

"Me?" The single word was rich with scorn. "You haven't heard of topographical maps? Satellite photos? GPS?"

He swallowed the dregs in his cup and casually got to his feet. He could see her tense, then slowly relax when he made no move toward her or the rifle she'd set aside. When he took a couple steps to the side, away from her, she relaxed even further.

That pulse in her throat hadn't slowed any, though. He found that…tantalizing.

"You and I both know that topo maps and satellite photos aren't much help in jungle like this." Derrick set the cup down on the crate of kitchenware. It was a natural move, and it left his hands free. He swung back to face her. "That's why I need *you.*"

She took a startled step back, away from him. Her hip hit the side of the table, making the dishes rattle. "I don't buy it. One man? To rescue just one hostage? Last I heard, the Sword had five or six hostages, not one."

"He's my brother." That came out sharper than he'd intended. Angrier. The anger made her bristle. She didn't seem to hear the guilt that wavered at the edges.

"Danny turned nineteen a week ago," he added flatly. "I don't imagine he had much of a celebration."

She wasn't backing down. "So you get your brother out, and other hostages are murdered in retaliation. I wouldn't call it a fair trade."

"Neither would I. But the Pilenau army is mounting a rescue operation. I know when and where they plan to hit. My goal is to be there just enough ahead of them to get Danny out without alerting the Sword. Then the army moves in and takes care of the rest of the hostages."

"So let them rescue your brother, too."

That was the last thing he wanted. The army wasn't likely to be any friendlier to Danny than the terrorists.

Derrick couldn't tell her that, but there was another explanation he knew she'd buy. It had the additional advantage of being absolutely true.

"The last time the army tried to hit the Sword," he said quietly, "it cost three hostages their lives. This time the good guys have an advantage. We know the layout of the camp. We know where the hostages are kept."

He hesitated, then added, "But he's my brother. And I've had training and experience the army hasn't. I won't willingly endanger the other hostages, but I won't leave him for someone else to rescue."

She studied him, unspeaking. Derrick couldn't tell what she was thinking, but the suddenly hollow look in her eyes said it wasn't about him. His words had triggered memories, and the memories had made her…vulnerable.

After a moment, she gave a reluctant sigh. "Show me what you plan."

She crossed to the bigger table, rummaged through several rolled maps at the side until she found what she wanted.

Derrick followed, careful not to glance at the rifle she'd left propped against the smaller table, which was now at his back. He scanned the papers and journals scattered on her worktable as she moved them out of the way, then picked up an ugly, twisted-looking plant with leathery leaves and gnarled, trailing roots. "What's this?"

She glanced up, looked away dismissively. *"Paphilopedilum bradshawensis.* An orchid. A rather ugly one, actually."

"Bradshawensis? Named after you?"

"My father."

He set the orchid aside. Even if he'd wanted to explore the subject further, the way she'd said *my father* made it clear discussion on that subject was at an end.

She picked up her coffee mug and casually tossed its contents on the ground, then plunked the cup down on an upper corner of the map. She used journals on two more corners, but smoothed the last corner flat with her hand.

Derrick, more aware of how close she was than he liked, bent over the map. She was the one who moved to put a few more inches of open air between them.

"Right now," he said, "the Sword's camped about five miles from here on a ridge near the Ipona River." He oriented himself to the map, then pointed. "There."

"You're sure?"

"I'm sure. I've seen the intelligence." He'd used every resource at his command to get it. Being a senior operative of Hudson opened a lot of doors. He'd gotten the rest however he could. Bribes. Connections. Friends of friends of friends. More bribes.

He thumped the spot on the map. "They're there. *Danny's* there."

She glanced at him, then back at the map. As she studied the twisting lines that portrayed the steep, rugged terrain he'd have to cross, her generous mouth turned down in a frown.

"If it were me, I'd fly in this way." She traced a deep valley that dug into the side of the massive, jungle-choked volcano that was Pilenau's heart. "If you kept low, no one would hear the helicopters. I'd land here—" she stabbed at the map with her right index finger "—or here, above the ridge. The jungle doesn't give you much room, but there are abandoned farms there where they could land.

Then it's downhill to the camp. Easier going than uphill, and faster."

Derrick, impressed, grunted assent. From what he'd heard, it had taken days for the so-called experts to agree on the army's approach. It had taken her sixty seconds to figure out the high points.

"That's pretty much what the army's planning," he admitted.

"When are they going to hit?"

"Two days from now. According to their sources, the bulk of the Sword will be away from camp, aiming to strike at the island's main port. The army plans to be there to welcome them. Their best chance of rescuing the hostages is while most of the Sword are out of camp, so they're coming this way, too. I'm not supposed to know that, of course," he added.

Her gaze came up to meet his. Her eyes, he discovered, were green.

No, not just green. They were the color of moss and shadow, with flecks of dull gold, like sunlight filtered through a canopy of leaves.

"So why," she asked, "are you on this side of the river with that ridge between you and the camp?"

The suspicion lacing her words brought his wandering thoughts up with a jerk. He held her gaze, willing her to believe him.

"Because you're here," he said.

Shadows darkened those incredible eyes.

"And because the last thing I want is to run the risk of alerting the Sword. They won't be expecting anyone coming at them from the river. Not with that ridge to protect them. Three miles long and damn near unclimbable. That's what I was told."

"And you're going to climb it?"

"Yes." He had to fight against the urge to touch her. "And you're going to help me."

He'd gone too far. Not a muscle in her face moved, yet her expression hardened, chilled. He had the sense that she'd withdrawn from him even though she was still close enough that he could smell the faint herbal scent of soap that lingered on her skin.

"All I need is for you to get me across that river, then show me the way up that ridge," he assured her. "That's all. Whatever your fee, I'll pay it. Hell, I'll double it! You won't get dragged in any farther, won't come close to any fighting. No one will even know you helped me. I promise. Just help me get to the top of that ridge before nightfall tomorrow. That's all I'm asking."

She might have been carved of stone for all the emotion he could see in her face.

"Please," he said, and winced at the hint of desperation in that single word. He drew a steadying breath, slowly let it out. "He's only nineteen."

Something flickered in her eyes, then vanished. Before he could decipher what he'd seen, she turned back to the map.

In profile, her face reminded him of the famous bust of the Egyptian queen, Nefertiti. An elegant head on a long, slender neck. The difference was, this woman was flesh and blood, not unfeeling stone. And whatever she was feeling right now had made her breathing go fast and a little bit shallow. The pulse in her throat was pounding even faster than before.

She smoothed back the corner of the map she was holding flat. Her hand looked longer, even more delicate, when it wasn't wrapped around the stock of a rifle.

"This is the best route to reach the river." She traced an invisible line along a cut that led up the side of the volcano, then across and back down to the river. "The first part's steep, but relatively easy going."

Again her gaze came up to meet his, coolly challenging. "Easy relative to most travel through these jungles, you understand. Which means it won't be easy at all."

He pointed to another cut where the topographic lines indicated the terrain wasn't so vertiginous. "Why not this way?"

"The stream that runs through there has produced extremely dense undergrowth. The other has no stream—it was cut off by a landslide upslope several years ago—so there's not so much foliage to hack your way through."

"Which still leaves a lot of jungle in the way," he said.

She shrugged. "Once up that cut, you stick to the game trails. They'll lead you across and back down to the river.

"The ridge on the other side of the river is the remnant of an old lava flow that got sliced away in an earthquake centuries ago," she continued, her low voice carefully steady. "It's almost vertical and the rock is fragile and unstable, very dangerous climbing. But there are two ways up. Here…and here."

Only one of the spots she'd indicated was close to the Sword's camp.

"It won't be easy. It's possible to make it to the top without climbing equipment. Harder with the weight you're carrying. Impossible at night."

"Not impossible. Nothing's impossible."

Except bringing back the dead.

But Danny wasn't going to die, so what did it matter?

"How long?"

"You'll have to be lucky, or extremely good, to get across the river and up that ridge before tomorrow night."

"I'm good," he said. "Damned good."

"But are you lucky?"

"I found you, didn't I?"

Silence, then, "I suppose you did."

The step he took toward her was completely involuntary.

"So you'll come?" he said, and tried to ignore the hope rising within him. "You'll help me rescue my brother?"

"Not a chance in hell," she said.

Chapter 2

From the moment Derrick Marx had triggered one of her crude but effective perimeter alarms, Elizabeth had known trouble was headed her way. The Pilenau jungle attracted too many men—they were always men—who knew far more about death and danger than any human should.

When Marx had stalked into her camp, rifle at the ready, she'd known he was one of them. He was a predator after prey, as at home as a jungle cat on the prowl.

When she'd dropped out of that old mango tree to confront him, she'd been prepared to run, if necessary, or shoot if she had to. But nothing had prepared her for the intensity of this particular man, the raw physical presence that made the hackles rise on the back of her neck even as she found herself responding to him.

As a scientist, she knew the reaction was an instinctive animal response to the presence of a predator, a female to a potent male. As a woman, she resented it intensely.

Her refusal to help had been automatic and equally instinctive. Pilenau's jungles were her refuge, her work here her salvation, but this man could all too easily disrupt the precarious peace she'd found here. She couldn't risk it. She didn't dare.

"I can't help you, Mr. Marx."

Marx wasn't a man who gave in easily. "I said I'd double your fee. Not bad pay for two day's work."

"I don't want your money."

His dark brows knotted in a frown. "I'm not asking you to lead me into their camp."

"I understand that."

"I'll protect you. Keep you safe. I swear."

The hackles rose higher. The man had no idea just how much he was asking of her. His brother... Her daughter... She caught her breath. She was damned if she was going to explain.

"I don't need your protection."

"But *I* need your knowledge."

"And I gave it to you."

She shoved aside the cup and journals holding the remaining three corners of the map, rolled it up and extended it to him.

"I've marked the main trails on this. You've got GPS. Nobody as well equipped as you are comes into the jungle without it," she added before he could lie.

"I don't need the map. I need *you*."

"You can't see the cut in the ridge from this side of the river," she continued as if he hadn't spoken. "It's hidden by an angle of rock and a heavy thicket of bamboo at the base. But it's there. You'll find it. There's enough of a path through the bamboo to show the way when you know to look for it."

When he still refused to take the map, she tossed it on the worktable. She wanted, suddenly, to touch him, to tell him that it would all work out somehow. And that made her want to turn and run.

Instead, she stood her ground and met his baleful glare.

Marx stared back, eyes hooded, jaw set hard under its stubble of beard. The local people who carved the faces of gods and monsters in stone might have used him as a model for one of the demon guardians of heaven, the pitiless creatures who judged the mortals standing at the gates seeking entrance to eternity.

Elizabeth couldn't help herself. She looked away.

Looking for a distraction, she picked up her cup, then pushed past him to replace the coffee he'd found so unpalatable.

Even with her back to him, she could *feel* him watching her.

"It's not the danger that's stopping you," he said.

She slammed down the half-filled cup, spun back to face him. "I don't like lies, Mr. Marx."

He tensed as though she'd struck him. "I haven't lied."

"I like half-truths even less."

His silence was as good as an admission.

She strode back to confront him. Anger, at least, was safe. She could keep on saying no if she was angry.

"What was your brother doing? Carrying drugs for the Sword, maybe? Buying wholesale with plans to do his own dealing? And don't tell me it wasn't something like that. You wouldn't be so damned worried about getting to him before the Pilenau army, otherwise. Not even knowing that this new rescue mission could go as badly wrong as the last one."

"He didn't mean—" His voice caught. He scowled, cleared his throat, tried again. "He's only nineteen."

"He's a fool. On Pilenau, even minor drug infractions carry horrible penalties if you're caught."

Elizabeth could see the cords in his neck tense.

"Which is why I need to get him out of that camp before the army gets there. He made mistakes. He doesn't deserve to pay for them with his life."

Beneath the anger she heard the love and the fear that drove Derrick Marx. She could sense the guilt.

She knew all about guilt.

Maybe—

No, dammit! She couldn't afford to risk it, couldn't afford to help. Not this man. Not *anyone*.

"The answer's still no."

"You've guided others, Dr. Bradshaw."

"Scientists. Adventurers. Search parties now and then. That's it. I've made a point of steering clear of the Sword and the drug dealers. And the army."

"Just across the river and up that cut."

"Take the map, Mr. Marx."

His only response was a hard-jawed silence.

When the silence stretched, Elizabeth pointedly turned back to her abandoned coffee. She forced herself to focus on the mundane tasks—topping up her cup, opening the sugar, picking up a spoon—and not on the man who stood four feet behind her. She was adding the first spoonful of sugar when she heard a familiar click behind her.

Elizabeth froze, cup in one hand, empty spoon in the other. Slowly, deliberately, she set down the cup and spoon, recapped the sugar, then, even more deliberately, turned to face him.

Marx had her rifle.

The safety was off. The muzzle pointed straight at her heart.

"I'm taking the map, Dr. Bradshaw," he said. "And I'm taking you with it."

Stupid, Bradshaw. Really stupid. You, of all people, ought to know you never let down your guard. Never, ever, ever.

Elizabeth slammed down on the familiar, accusing voice in her head.

"A word of advice, Dr. Bradshaw. The next time a heavily armed man walks into your camp, run, don't talk."

"Next time, I'll remember that. For now…"

Two steps divided her from potential extinction. Elizabeth never took her eyes off his as she crossed that small space. She didn't bother to look down when she placed her fingertip at the business end of the rifle.

The silent war of wills between them stretched, then fractured. Elizabeth knew she'd won when the faint lines of tension tugging on his lower eyelids eased.

She calmly pushed the rifle aside, away from her heart.

"Here's some advice for you, Marx—guns only work if the person on the other end is convinced you might actually use them."

His lower lip pushed out in the resigned grimace of

a poker player who's just had his bluff called. He shrugged, then handed her the rifle.

"Never hurts to try."

She'd reset the safety when alarm bells started going off in her head. For a man who'd just lost, he was way too calm.

She flipped the safety off again and backed up a step, the rifle cradled in her hands and pointing at him.

"I'm not going with you."

His only response was a smile. Difference was, this smile had teeth.

She took another step back. "What?"

For answer, he tugged open a Velcro flap on a pocket at his thigh and pulled out a satellite phone. Still smiling, he punched a button, then listened as the call went through. Even from three feet away she could hear the beeps and buzzes as electronic relays a mile up and half a world away connected.

"Bear," he said when the call connected, "got a lady wants to talk to you."

Marx held out the phone. "Friend of mine named Bear Gerofsky. I saved his hide a few years ago so he's always willing to help when I need a favor." When she hesitated, he added, "You definitely want to talk to him, Dr. Bradshaw."

The smile was gone, the threat now unmistakable.

Elizabeth's stomach hollowed out. She shifted her grip on the rifle—she could use it one-handed if she had to—and reluctantly took the phone.

"Mr. Gerofsky."

"Mizz Bradshaw." The voice had the harsh rasp of a heavy smoker. "Marx thought you'd like to know about this kid we're watchin'. Neeng. Nang. Somethin' like that."

The earth shifted dizzily beneath her feet. "Niang."

"That's the one. Him an' his father, they carry your mail, right? Deliver supplies?"

Marx was watching her, stone-faced, distant. Waiting.

"Yes." She could barely breathe.

"Way we hear it, you're kinda fond of the kid."

For an instant, she stopped breathing altogether.

"*Real* fond. You get my drift?"

Her silence didn't seem to trouble him. "In case you think we're just yankin' your chain, the guy we got watchin' him says this Niang's wearing some baggy blue shorts and an old gray T-shirt today. Shirt says somethin' about biologists an' birds an' bees."

Elizabeth's hand closed convulsively around the phone. It was Niang's favorite shirt. She'd given it to him last year after a science team she'd worked with had left it behind.

"Nice kid," Gerofsky added casually. "Shame if anythin' happened to him."

The words sounded so commonplace, like an offhand comment dropped in casual conversation.

"For God's sake, he's only eleven years old!"

"Life's a bitch, Doc. Little kids get hurt all the time, right? Even killed."

Oh, God! Oh, God, oh, God, oh, God! The words spun in her head, a horrified prayer. They knew. About her. About Shanna. They *knew!* Oh, God… *Niang!*

"All the kids in the world, Doc," her tormentor added softly, "what's one more or less?"

Elizabeth snatched the phone from her ear. Marx took it before she could fling it away. He shut it off, then shoved it back in his thigh pocket.

"What was that you said earlier, Dr. Bradshaw? Something about guns only work if you're convinced the other guy might really use them?"

"Bastard." It was barely a whisper, but it carried all the fear and hate welling within her.

She didn't resist when he took her rifle from her.

"You'll want to start packing," he said. "We've got a lot of ground to cover, and we don't have much time to do it."

The *parang* bit into the strangling vine with such force that Elizabeth could feel the shock all the way up her shoulder. The angled blade sank halfway through the tough, six-inch-thick fibrous stem, then jammed.

She yanked the blade free, then struck again.

Like a vast curtain torn free of its supports, the vine arced downward, sweeping in front of her to dangle from its remaining anchorage in a quivering mass of green. One last blow cut it free. Despite her uncertain footing, Elizabeth savagely kicked it to the side, out of the way.

The muscles in her arms, shoulders and back ached from hours of hacking a way through raw jungle. She wouldn't have made it this far this fast if it hadn't been for the churning mix of fury and fear driving her. Imagining that it was Marx or his bearish pal, Gerofsky, falling beneath every cutting blow had helped.

She swiped a sweaty forearm across her brow, then, arm trembling from exertion, slipped the *parang* back in its carrying loop and tugged her water bottle out of its pocket. The water was warm and carried the chemical taste of rehydration salts and iodine.

Even in a jungle that got more than two hundred inches of rain a year, dehydration was a constant risk for anyone engaged in heavy physical activity. Stifling heat like this, with every drop of sweat you lost precious body salts and minerals. Lose enough and it didn't matter how much water you drank, you were in a coma. Or dead.

She deliberately hadn't bothered to check if Marx had enough water, or if he carried the necessary water purifiers and packets of salts.

Elizabeth forced herself to take another swallow, then replaced the half-empty bottle. They'd been slogging through dense, heavily overgrown jungle for almost five hours now, but had covered less than two miles of the five or six that divided them from the terrorists' camp.

It wasn't that she'd been dawdling. In this green hell those two miles had meant fighting their way up treacherously steep slopes through jungle growth that seemed to spring up right in front of them. Trees whose tops were invisible through the tangle of vines and ferns and foliage kept the jungle floor in eternal twilight. The dim light made it hard to see the rough volcanic rock and twining roots that could break an ankle, or the tiny, poisonous tree frogs that could kill a man.

So far, Marx had eluded the traps that Pilenau set for the unwary.

Elizabeth glanced back. The man was maybe thirty feet downslope from her, still fighting his way through a treacherous knot of creepers and fallen branches. If he'd been a few feet lower, the trees crowding the narrow defile would have hidden him completely. As it was, the slope was so steep that she could see the top of the soft-brimmed jungle hat he wore but not his face.

While she watched, he heaved himself over a downed tree, then stopped, panting, propped one foot on a rock and braced his hand against his knee to help support the weight of the pack he carried.

The pack worried her. He clearly knew enough about jungle travel not to carry an ounce more in supplies and equipment than he absolutely needed. For three, even four days' travel, especially when he had to travel fast, he didn't need that much. So why the big pack? What was he carrying that was worth the effort of hauling it up a slope like this?

It wouldn't be food. Modern communications and GPS equipment were neither bulky nor heavy. Medical supplies, maybe?

But that didn't make sense. If this rescue mission was going to succeed he had to get his brother out of the camp and onto that helicopter as quickly as possible. The last thing he'd want was to spend time on anything more than absolutely essential first aid.

Besides, he hadn't said anything about his brother being ill or injured, just that he knew where— She frowned, trying to remember the boy's name. Danny?

He'd said he knew where Danny was being held, but he hadn't mentioned any injuries.

Not medical supplies, then.

Which left weapons and ammunition.

But so much? For one man? That didn't make sense, either.

Marx glanced up. Even at this distance his gaze carried a hostile punch that rocked right through her.

Without a word, he carefully picked his way up the intervening slope toward her. Despite the heat and the weight he carried, the brief rest had allowed him to catch his breath. He made the difficult climb look almost easy. And that just pissed her off more.

Elizabeth considered setting off again, keeping that safe distance between them while wearing him down. He wanted to get to the ridge above the Ipona as fast as possible. She wanted to get him the hell out of her life— and Niang's—even faster, so why not oblige?

Trouble was, the safe distance between them ever since they'd left camp was beginning to feel more like cowardice than strategy.

She stood her ground.

He was almost level with her when one of the jagged volcanic rocks hidden in the smothering green shifted under her weight, throwing her off balance.

His hand shot out, clamping around her arm like a vise.

"Steady, Doc. You're not much good to me with a broken ankle."

Elizabeth could feel the calluses on his palm, the strength in those long fingers. Her skin burned at the contact. Nobody had touched her for a long, long time. *Nobody*.

She angrily tugged free of his grip, wavered, then found her balance.

"Don't call me Doc."

He was a few inches below her. It wouldn't take much of a shove to send him tumbling down the hill. People died in easier falls all the time. A place like this—

His eyes narrowed. "Don't even think it. You try, I'll take you with me, and then where would little Niang be?"

She jerked back, upper lip lifting in an animal snarl. "There's a special place in hell for people like you."

"Maybe so. But hell will have to wait until I've got my brother safe."

And then he brushed past her as if she weren't even there, climbing higher, away from her.

As he passed, the edge of his pack knocked her shoulder, throwing her back off balance. Elizabeth's foot slipped, her ankle twisted. If she hadn't instinctively flung herself forward, into the hillside above her, she'd have toppled over backward instead.

The shock as her knee and thrusted-out hand slammed onto exposed lava dragged an involuntary gasp out of her.

For what seemed like forever, she simply crouched there, shoulders hunched, fingers digging into the un-yielding rock, fighting against the sharp, hot tears of mingled pain and fury and frustration and fear that threatened. Her body already ached from the brutally swift hike up the mountain. Now her palm and knee burned. It wouldn't be long before they'd be throbbing like hell. And the man who was the cause of it all hadn't even bothered looking back.

She should have shoved him down the mountain when she'd had the chance.

A glance at her shredded knee brought a string of curses in English and fluent Pilenauan. She needed to clean and disinfect the wounds—in the jungle even a minor cut could turn septic dangerously fast—but that could wait for now.

Above her, Marx clambered over a fallen log, then up an exposed spine of rock. She might as well have not existed for all the heed he paid her.

He'd won this round. She wouldn't let him win another. For Niang's sake, she didn't dare risk leading him the long way around or, more tempting, abandoning him altogether. But that didn't mean she couldn't make the next forty-eight hours some of the most miserable of his long, miserable life.

Gritting her teeth against the rising chorus of complaints from her battered body, Elizabeth set off up the hill after him.

Chapter 3

The last thirty feet were damn near straight up. Cursing, fingers and booted toes scrabbling for leverage, Derrick inched his way up the wall of black rock. It must have been a hell of a waterfall before that landslide Bradshaw had mentioned. He'd hate to have tackled the climb if there'd been tons of water sailing past him.

A foot below the top he paused, listening, then slowly pulled himself up to peer over the edge. Nothing there but more rock and a hell of a lot more jungle.

With one last effort he heaved himself over the rim to lie there, belly down, lungs heaving. Amazing how appealing flat ground was when you hadn't seen any for hours.

Once his heart rate slowed, he shucked his pack and the rifle he'd strapped to it and shoved them aside, then leaned back over the edge to check on Bradshaw's progress.

She was still about six feet down, moving confidently but with care along a route that had kept her out of any falling rocks he might have inadvertently launched. They hadn't exchanged one word since that ugly little confrontation on the hillside.

He watched as she picked her way along a fissure in the rock face, then up another foot. Once, he saw her grab for a handhold, then snatch her hand back, shaking it as if it stung. The second time she was more wary, testing the rock before digging her fingers in for a better grip. She was in better shape than he was, more at home in this damned jungle, but still...

He stretched out flat, then leaned over the edge, hand extended. "Want some help?"

She tilted her head up, startled, giving him a good look at her face. The expression there made him withdraw his hand.

"Right." He got to his feet. "Let me know if you change your mind."

He shifted pack and rifle farther back to give her more room, then, muscles protesting, gratefully slumped to the ground beside them. For a moment he just sat there, head tilted back, eyes closed, savoring the lack of dragging weight on his shoulders.

A clatter of falling pebbles announced Bradshaw's arrival at the top. He reluctantly opened his eyes and sat up, ready to offer his help if she wanted it.

Her hand appeared first, blindly groping for a solid hold, then the crown of her canvas slouch hat. A moment later, she got an elbow hooked over the edge.

The look she shot him would have melted steel.

To hell with it. Derrick leaned back against his pack,

stretched out his legs, laced his hands behind his head and stared up into the intricate tracery of leaves above his head. Right now, not moving, ever, sounded like a hell of a fine idea. That and an ice-cold beer. Or three.

Bradshaw inched her way over the top. Once up, she simply crouched at the edge, head down, hands braced on the ground to help support the weight she carried, breathing hard.

He should have helped her up.

She'd probably have pulled him over the edge if he'd tried. Thirty-foot fall, sharp-edged rocks at the bottom. Place like this, the insects would have his carcass picked clean in a week. A couple of years, only the heavy nylon webbing on his pack, a few bits of bones and the rusted steel of his weapons would still be around to mark where he'd fallen.

Luckily for him, she was too smart, and too worried about the little friend of hers that Bear had convinced her they'd staked out to try anything that stupid.

There'd be hell to pay once she realized they'd lied, that they'd tricked her into helping, but he didn't have the energy to worry about that now.

At the moment what they both needed was water, rest and food. In that order.

Had Danny had any food today? Any water?

The thought made him jerk upright, suddenly ashamed. While he sat here complaining, Danny was lying in a bamboo cage barely large enough to hold his lanky, not-quite-grown body. The cage was in a grass hut on a ridge that still lay miles to the north of here.

Every minute he wasted was one more minute that Danny suffered, one less minute that he had for getting his brother out before the Pilenau army moved in.

"You sure there wasn't an easier route up?" he demanded.

Without wasting a glance on him, Bradshaw rocked back on her heels, tilted her head back to ease the strain on her neck, then forward. "You didn't say *easy,* you said *fast.* And that's exactly what you got."

She swatted at a mosquito on her arm. The sound of flesh hitting flesh rang like a gunshot on the still air. She scowled at the streak of mashed bug and blood on her arm, then grimly wiped it away.

"Stop whining, Marx. I'll get you where you want to go as fast as humanly possible." She raised her head, those dark eyes pinning him in place. "For Niang's sake, not yours."

When he kept silent, she tugged off her rifle and pack, then shoved to her feet and dragged everything to the opposite side of the old streambed, as far away from him as she could get.

Even dirty, sweat-soaked and bug-bitten, she looked good. Even tired she moved with an economical grace that caught a man's eye. Another time, under different circumstances…

Derrick watched as she retrieved her water bottle from its pocket on one side of the pack, a small plastic box from a pocket on the other. The little grunt she made as she flopped on the ground was followed by a muffled, weary sigh.

Guilt stabbed at him. Despite his assurances to the contrary, he knew he was taking her in harm's way. She'd probably forgive him for that far more readily than she'd forgive him for the lies he and Bear had told her.

Not that it mattered. With luck, by the time she realized how he and Bear had played on her known affection for Niang—a boy they'd learned about from an informer but never seen—Danny would be safe and on his way home. Saving Danny was what mattered. What she thought of him didn't.

He watched as she tilted the water bottle over the open palm of her right hand. It was her wince as the water hit her palm, the small, stifled grunt of pain, that brought him to his feet. He was across the clearing in three long strides.

The sight of her raw, bloody palm and bloodier knee dropped him to his knees in front of her. Before she could object, he grabbed her right wrist and forced her fingers to uncurl.

The heel of her hand had taken the worst of it, though there were ragged, bloody scrapes all the way across her palm. Even under the crusting blood he could see jagged bits of lava half-buried in the exposed flesh. Her knee was in even worse shape.

"Damn it to hell!" The words exploded out of him. "When did you do this?"

She snatched her hand back, furious. "When you knocked me over back there on that hillside."

"*I* knocked you over!"

"That's right! You and that damn big pack of yours.

If I hadn't had the good sense to fall forward, I'd have gone over backward and broken my neck, instead!"

He blinked, shaken. Instinctively, he stretched out his hand to touch her in a wordless apology, and just as quickly drew it back. She'd probably bite it off. Worse, he didn't trust himself. He *wanted* to touch her.

"I'm sorry. You should have said—"

"What? And kept you from playing hero by delaying this insane quest of yours? I wouldn't dream of it!"

"Do you have any idea how fast something like this can get infected here?"

"No. Why would I? I've only lived here most of my life."

Derrick opened his mouth to retort but gave a wry grimace and rocked back on his heels, instead. He gestured to the plastic box she'd pulled from her pack. "Got any disinfectant in that? Or a pair of tweezers?"

She held her injured hand to her chest protectively. "I can take care of myself."

"That's not what I asked." When she didn't reply, he picked up the box and flipped up its lid. "Pretty tidy little collection here. Gauze. Sutures. Needle. Adhesive bandages. Hmmm… Aspirin. Antihistamines. What's this?" He held up a clear plastic bottle containing a pale green liquid.

"Topical antibiotic made from medicinal plants. I buy it from the local healer."

"Does it work?"

Her lips thinned. "What do you think?"

"I'll take that as a yes." He set the bottle at his feet

and went back to rummaging among the box's neatly packed, plastic-wrapped contents.

"Here we are. Tweezers." He closed the box, set it aside. "Give me your hand."

She clutched it tighter to her chest. "I can take care of myself."

"I'm sure you can," he said mildly. Strangling her wouldn't do either one of them much good. "But you're right-handed, so guess which hand you stuck out to catch your fall."

If looks could kill, he'd be in his death throes right now.

"I'm just going to pick out the bits of lava," he said, not quite so mildly this time. "If you think you can do it better left-handed than I can with two good hands, you can have the tweezers."

She just glared at him across the invisible barrier of mistrust and animosity that divided them.

He glared back. "Stop being so damned stupid!"

She balled up her fist to clobber him, winced and reluctantly gave in.

"Fine!" She thrust out her hand, palm up.

He cradled her hand in his, pinning her fingers open with his thumb. Her fingers were long, slender, more delicate than he'd realized. He could feel the hard lines of bones beneath his fingertips, the softer, yielding ridges of veins that lay just beneath the surface of her sweat-slicked skin.

Her palm, especially the fleshy mound at the base of her thumb, was a mess.

He sloshed more water over the wound; then, as

gently as he could, peeled off the hardening crust of clotted blood. Not gently enough. Her fingers twitched; her breath caught, ever so faintly.

"Sorry."

"I'm fine." She said it between gritted teeth. "Just get on with it."

Fortunately, the wound wasn't deep. Unfortunately, the black, volcanic rock she'd struck had left a lot of pieces behind. Removing the forming scab had started blood flowing again. That helped wash out the wound but hid the tiny stones he was hunting. Each probe brought an involuntary flinch, an occasional hiss of sharply indrawn breath, but she didn't try to pull away.

Eventually, he released her hand. His own hands were alive with the remembered feel of hers. "Best I can do for now."

She flexed her fingers, wincing slightly. She didn't waste her breath on thanks.

He handed her the plastic bottle of her local miracle potion. "Rinse that off while I take care of your knee."

"I can—"

"Take care of it yourself. I know. Rinse it off and stop arguing."

He bent to take a closer look at her abused knee.

"Looks like hell. Why didn't you say something sooner?"

She didn't bother answering that question.

He plucked an ugly bit of gravel from the wound,

ignored her stifled gasp of pain, then sloshed more
water on her knee, flushing the wound. As gently as he
could, he pulled off the scab forming over the gravel
and raw flesh.

She flinched.

"Sorry."

The scab came off. The gravel was tougher. He
frowned, leaning closer still, trying to spot the bits of
black beneath the welling blood and serum. Without
thinking, he wrapped his free hand around the back of
her knee, holding her steady.

Her skin was hot, damp with sweat and roughened by
bug bites, fresh scratches, dirt and mashed bits of greenery.

It was all he could do not to run his palm along the
smooth, strong curve of her calf, or trace the delicate
line of bone to where it disappeared in her boot.

She'd have beautiful feet. He was sure of it. Slender
and shapely, just like her hands.

As if sensing his sharp awareness of her, she tried
to jerk free.

"Hold still, dammit!"

"I could do it faster."

"You could have done it earlier, too. But you didn't,
so I'm in charge now."

He got a better grip on the tweezers, lowered his
head to focus on what he was doing.

A bit of gravel. Another. A scrap of green. It had to
hurt like hell.

After one particularly bad moment, he glanced up to
find her, head bent, blindly scowling at him, the un-

opened bottle of green goop in her other hand, clearly forgotten.

Her breathing had gone fast and a little shallow, but not from the pain. He stifled a small smile of satisfaction.

"You going to pour that stuff on your hand or just admire the mess?"

She jumped, startled and transferred the scowl from her palm to him. "I'm letting it air."

Derrick eyed the bottle dubiously. "You sure about that stuff? I've got antibiotic cream if—"

"I'm sure." She gave the bottle a shake, flipped the top open with her thumb.

Derrick couldn't help himself. He stared, his attention caught by her open palm, the angle of her arm, the line of hand and wrist and elbow.

Bradshaw raised the bottle, tipped it. He waited for her to tip it farther, waited for the liquid to pour out over her palm, run down her wrist.

She paused, bottle still poised over her hand, her gaze fixed on him.

"Either finish with my knee, Marx," she said pointedly, "or let go of it. I'm not going anywhere."

Derrick jerked, let go of her knee, almost dropped the tweezers.

"Sorry. I was wondering what that stuff was."

That was a lie. He hadn't been thinking at all.

"Some local plant extracts. Water. Ground up bug guts, for all I know," she snapped. "*I* don't know what's in it. Neither do the three different university labs that have studied it. Not for sure. I just know it works, okay?"

Derrick took a deep breath. "Sure. I was just... wondering."

"Well, stop wondering and start finishing with my knee. Or back off and let me do it myself."

"Touchy, aren't you?"

"No. I'm tired, filthy, hungry, sore and royally pissed. At you, Marx, in case you were wondering. I don't want you touching me. I don't want you *near* me. I don't even want you in my *jungle*. But if you cleaning up my knee will get it done faster, I'm all for it, because what I *do* want is to get you the hell out of my life, and Niang's life, as quickly as possible. Got it?"

"Got it."

"Good."

She gave the bottle another vicious shake and turned her attention back to her hand.

Derrick set the tweezers aside and slopped water on her knee. Her problem if she got an infection, not his. She should have said something when he'd knocked her over, dammit.

That roused the guilt again. And once again he shoved it down.

With a hunk of gauze, he swabbed away the worst of the watery blood trickling down her leg, then rocked back on his heels.

"That's it. All I could get, anyway."

She glanced at his handiwork, then shifted to douse it with the magic green stuff. "I've had worse."

She probably had, Derrick thought, watching her. Living and working alone as she did in a place like this, she had to be used to relying on herself, on her own inner strengths as well as the limited medical resources available to her.

He thought of the sealed packets of sutures and needles and gauze he'd seen in her medical kit. His Special Forces training had included what to do in case of serious injury far from help. But behind that training there was always the assumption, often unspoken, that help would be coming. Helicopters, rescue teams, whatever it took. If a man went down, he knew that others would risk their lives to get him out.

Elizabeth Bradshaw couldn't count on any of that, ever. He'd seen the hand-crank emergency radio in her camp. It wasn't something you'd take in the jungle with you, especially if you had to carry it on your back. He'd watched her load her pack. She didn't have a satellite phone like the one he carried. Once she was away from camp, she was on her own and out of touch. If she broke a leg instead of just scraping her knee, there'd be no one to splint it, no one to go for help or carry her back down the mountain. If she fell while climbing, if she suffered a really serious injury, she'd die here, and she'd die alone.

What kind of woman—what kind of human being—not only sought such isolation, but guarded it as Bradshaw guarded hers? What had driven her to choose a life like this? And why?

They weren't the kind of questions he could ask or that she'd ever answer.

She was done with her knee. She recapped the bottle, tucked it back in the kit he'd left open on the ground beside her, then rearranged the mess he'd made, setting things back in their proper place. Neat. Tidy. A woman who liked things ordered and under control in a world where the land itself ran riot.

It was a contradiction that he found…intriguing.

He shoved to his feet.

"That's good enough," he said roughly. "We'll rest when we reach the river and can refill the water bottles."

Bradshaw tensed but chose to ignore him. With careful precision she snapped the first aid kit shut, returned it to its pocket, smoothed the Velcro flap in place, then, one by one, checked every strap and flap and pocket on her pack. She never once looked up at him, never by so much as a blink of an eyelash acknowledged that he existed.

It was deliberate provocation, and it was working. He could feel his temper rising.

"Help me up." It wasn't a request.

Surprised, he took her outstretched left hand and pulled her to her feet—and she damned near pulled him off his.

He barely stopped the instinctive reaction to drop, to pull her down with him, then flip her over the edge of the cliff and onto the rocks below. He tightened his grip on her hand. Instead of letting go, she yanked him closer, as close as lovers angling for a kiss…or boxers moving in for a brutal body blow.

Her eyes had narrowed to slits. They glittered, black and dangerous, mere inches from his.

"In this jungle, Marx, I'm the one giving the orders, not you. Understand?"

He held her gaze, increased the pressure of his grip on her hand. It had to hurt. She didn't back off an inch.

He let go of her hand. "Trick like that, Bradshaw, I could have tossed you over the edge. If I didn't need you so damn much, I might have done it, too."

"Yeah? Well the fact is, you need me. And little though I like it, you've got me until I get you across that river and point the way up that cliff. You get to the top of that cliff, you can go to hell for all I care, but until then, until you call your dogs off Niang, you'll do what I say, when I say it, because I don't want even the slightest chance of your screwing things up."

She didn't ask if he understood. She didn't ask if he agreed. She simply pinned him with that dark, glittering gaze. And then she roughly shoved him back.

That caught him off guard, too. He staggered, swore, caught his balance.

She was already slipping her arms through the straps on her pack, picking up her rifle. She was still adjusting the pack when she ducked under an overhanging branch and disappeared.

It was only as he was settling his own pack into place that he realized she'd shoved him away with the flat of her injured hand. There, atop the breast pocket of his shirt, almost invisible in the camouflage pattern of greens and browns, was the print of her palm, etched in blood right over his heart.

Chapter 4

Ten minutes later, they hit the game trail Bradshaw had sketched on her map. The trail itself stopped Derrick dead in his tracks.

"It's a damned highway!" he snarled, glaring at the broad, well-worn path that cut through the jungle.

She shrugged. "Elephants take up a little more space than the rest of us."

He turned his glare on her. "Elephants?"

"It's the main trail they use to get to the Ipona. They don't cross the river there since there's nowhere for them to go, but they do use the shallows of the ford for bathing."

"From the looks of it, it's not just elephants that use this trail."

"No. Elephants make good trails. Everything else in the jungle just takes advantage of them. Including humans." She shifted the sling on her rifle higher up her shoulder. "*Especially* humans."

"So what made *those* tracks?" he demanded, pointing.

"A *pelanduk*—a mouse deer." She studied the scuffed markings. "Three of them, actually. I've seen wild boar along here and a leopard once. Occasionally, I'll find the tracks of a tiger."

"Lions and tigers and bears, oh my!"

"*Tigers,* Marx. Not lions and bears."

So she'd never seen *The Wizard of Oz.* She got the sarcasm just fine.

Maybe, when all this was over, when he had Danny and she realized her little friend was safe, he'd talk her into letting him show her some of the things she'd missed. After years in this damned jungle, she was due a little vacation. Hell! He *owed* her one!

Of course, there were all sorts of ways to vacation.

He thought of his big-screen TV, his one real indulgence, and the broad, extraordinarily comfortable leather sofa in front of it. They wouldn't even have to put in a movie if they didn't want to....

The jolt of heat that thought roused brought him back to the present with a vicious snap.

"Judging from how well traveled this trail is," he said sourly, "you might as well send out announcements that we're here."

Her jaw jutted dangerously. "If you came through the village where Niang lives—and you had to, to get to me—then half of Pilenau already knows you're here. But they'll figure you're either some scientist working with me or one of those crazy adventure travelers looking for a guide. Nobody would dream you're crazy enough to tackle the Sword."

I hope. She didn't say it. She didn't have to.

When he didn't respond, she gave an angry hitch to

her shoulders, then spun on her heel and marched away, leaving him to fall into step behind her.

"Whatever you're thinking," he said, "don't."

"Maybe it was something nice."

"I'm sure you thought so." When she kept silent, he added, amused, "Haven't you been counting up the number of ways you could…err…eliminate me? Jungle like this, there's gotta be a hundred easy ways to do it."

Bradshaw stopped so abruptly, he almost ran into her.

"The native peoples of Pilenau have words for the numbers one through ten," she said, holding up her hands, fingers spread, just to annoy him. "After that, they settle for the equivalent of many. Or many many if they have a whole lot more than ten."

"And you got to…what? Many many many?"

"I'm a little better at math than the Pilenauans." She gave him a smile that had a warning twist in it. "In my doctoral dissertation on the poisons concocted by the native tribes here, I identified twenty-seven separate compounds. Most of them fairly easy to produce."

"That's nice. So how many of them are lethal?"

She smiled. "All of them, Marx," she said. "Every last one of them."

The trail was wide enough for two, but Derrick wasn't any more interested in conversation than Bradshaw was. Grateful for the easier going, he kept a good distance between them and tried not to think about Danny.

The trouble was, not thinking about Danny left him not much of anything else to think about except *her*. That and watch those long, slim legs walk away from him, which didn't do anything to improve his mood, either.

Elizabeth Bradshaw, Ph.D., was proud, prickly and downright unfriendly. Not that she had any cause for friendliness, but he had the feeling she'd have been much the same if he'd strolled into camp bearing gifts rather than threats. And yet...

The hotter and more tired he got, the more easily he could imagine a woman far different from the sweat-streaked, mud-splattered, angry one in front of him.

It was, in fact, disconcertingly easy to imagine her dressed in some slinky, sexy red number that hugged the curves even her practical khakis couldn't hide. Something cut low at the top and all the way up to there at the bottom. Something that shimmered in the light.

He could picture her hair down about her shoulders, shining and soft and swinging with every long, confident step she took. Despite the ugly boots and heavy socks, he could easily picture her, slender feet poised atop insanely high high heels. The blood-stirring, nothing-much-there kind of heels with one of those thin leather straps that fastened around the ankle. The kind that was so intriguing to take off...or maybe leave on when everything else came off.

It took no effort whatsoever to picture her wearing nothing at all. *That* image came through nice and clear.

On the trail ahead of him, Bradshaw decapitated an encroaching vine with one vicious stroke of her *parang*.

Derrick grimaced. So much for imagination.

Still, he couldn't help wondering why a woman with

her education and abilities would choose to live in a place like this, even if she did know twenty-seven different ways to kill a man but had never seen *The Wizard of Oz*.

She'd come back five years ago. He knew that much. After a childhood spent on Pilenau with a brilliant, reclusive father who, after the death of his wife, had refused to leave the jungle, she'd escaped at last to the States and a stellar university career. She'd married some professor she'd met at Harvard and started making a name for herself in the academic world. Then, suddenly, she wasn't married and she was back on Pilenau, alone. It was a tale that left a hell of a lot of gaps, and a hell of a lot more questions.

Given the limited time available to him, Derrick hadn't thought it important to find out more. He'd dug just deep enough to be sure she was the best person to help him get to Danny, and then he'd dug a little deeper for the information that would ensure she *did* help him, whether she wanted to or not.

Not that it mattered now. He'd done what he had to do. For Danny. Because he'd had no choice.

But there was still room for regret, and time, while he watched those long legs cover the ground ahead of him, to indulge in it.

Derrick caught the smell of running water long before he heard the gurgle and slap of it flowing over rock. The sweet scent, barely discernible above the heavy, earthy smells of the jungle around them, brought a renewed burst of energy. Ahead of him, Bradshaw had already lengthened her stride.

The trail curved around a clump of palms, ducked beneath a massive mango tree, then widened into a clearing bisected by a stream whose mossy banks couldn't quite hide the tracks of the wild creatures that had passed there and paused to drink. At the sight of human intruders, a white-and-cream-colored hornbill burst into startled flight, temporarily abandoning its fishing expedition.

Derrick stopped dead, startled by the overwhelming beauty of the place.

Tumbled black rocks hemmed a pool of shadowed green and silver fed by a twenty-foot waterfall that plunged down an almost vertical wall of volcanic rock. On the far side of the pool, a tangle of ferns and purple-spotted orchids softened the rocky sides while a flock of iridescent yellow butterflies danced in the air overhead, oblivious to any intruders. Around it all, like living castle walls, vine-laced trees reared skyward, keeping the world at bay. The scent of a wild plum tree in bloom drifted like perfume in the air.

Eden must have been like this before Adam and Eve ruined things for everyone.

He glanced over at Bradshaw. She stood, rapt, as caught by the beauty of it as he was.

For the first time since she'd dropped out of that tree, rifle in hand, she'd forgotten about him, forgotten everything but the miracle of the world before her. There was a softness to her features he'd never seen before. And something else, something… He groped for the words.

Sadness, he thought. And regret. And…longing? But for what?

As if sensing his gaze, Bradshaw shook herself out of her introspection.

"We'll fill up the water bottles here." She glanced up at a sky whose blue had long since faded to a formless cottony-gray. "Rain's coming. Once it starts, it's not going to stop. Best to make camp soon, before it gets too dark."

"Not here. Not near running water."

"Like to hear your enemy sneaking up on you, Marx?"

"Don't you?" This time, when he scanned the walls of green hemming them in, he wasn't looking at the beauty. "It's a good place for an ambush. Dense jungle or steep rock walls on all sides. And as far as I can see, there's only one way out—that damned elephant highway of yours."

As if to mock their human concerns, a kingfisher, its plumage an almost metallic blue against the green, darted over the stream then was gone an instant later.

Bradshaw slipped off her pack and set it down on a flat rock at the water's edge, then knelt to tug her water bottles free of the mesh pockets that held them.

"We need water," she said. "Unless you want to go thirsty, you'll fill up here. There won't be another good spot for it until the Ipona."

Derrick hesitated, then shook his head. "Better if you refill all our bottles while I stand guard. Please," he added when her eyes narrowed dangerously.

For a moment he thought she'd refuse. Instead, she gave a curt nod and rose to her feet. "Turn around."

He carried one bottle in a pouch on his belt, where it was easy to reach. The rest, like hers, were behind him in pockets at the sides of his pack. To reach them, he'd have to remove the pack. It simply made sense for her to retrieve them, instead. Faster and easier, all the way around.

But not nearly so smart.

He could see her, head bent, just at the edge of his vision. He could hear the rip of Velcro, sense the slight tug as she pulled the first bottle free, then the second. Just a tug, yet he could feel the shift of weight, the almost imperceptible pull of the straps at his shoulder, chest and waist. He breathed in, startled at the unexpected...*intimacy* of it.

She tucked the two bottles in the crook of her arm and moved to his left side, still behind him. Another rip of Velcro, another tug.

Damned jungle was getting to him. *She* was getting to him.

"Purification tablets?" she demanded curtly, moving to stand in front of him, left hand out, palm up. She held her right arm across her chest, pinning the water bottles against her breasts. Given her injured hand, it was an obvious, eminently practical way to carry the awkward bottles, yet Derrick found himself staring.

"Marx?" she insisted. "You have any purification tablets or rehydration salts? Or were you planning on taking your chances with whatever parasites and bacteria are floating in that stuff?"

With a silent oath, he yanked himself back to attention.

Careful not to meet her gaze, he dug in one of the half dozen pockets on his shirt. He almost dropped the handful of foil packets he pulled out. Under that unblinking stare, his fingers suddenly seemed too big and far too clumsy.

"Rehydration salts," he said, dumping the packets in her hand. "Make sure you use some, too. The bottles have purification filters built into the lids."

When she didn't move, he looked up. "What?"

Her fingers curled over the packets. "Nothing."

"You were hoping I'd collapse of heat exhaustion, maybe?"

"No." She started to turn away, then stopped. Her chin came up. "Not yet, anyway."

There was no mistaking her meaning. "Nothing's going to happen to Niang, I swear. No one's going to hurt him. I just—" He caught himself. He didn't dare admit to the lies about Niang. "Get me up that cliff and you won't have to worry. About anything."

"Really?" The sarcasm was sharp enough to cut.

With ruthless efficiency, she lined up both their water bottles on a broad, flat rock at the edge of the pool, then, one by one, ripped open the packets of rehydration salts and dumped them in, one packet for each liter bottle. She'd shut him out as efficiently as if she'd pulled a door shut between them, yet Derrick found himself watching her instead of keeping his attention on the jungle around them.

He couldn't help himself, couldn't help noticing the neat economy of motion as she bent to dip an empty bottle in the pool, the curve of her back and tilt of her head as she waited for the bottle to fill, the easy grace with which she lifted the filled bottle, then turned to tip its contents into one of the waiting empties.

Crouched like that, she'd left the nape of her neck exposed. Tiny curls at the hairline, too short to be pulled into that ugly ponytail, lay damply against her skin. Above the sweat-dampened collar of her shirt, he could see the knob of a vertebra where her neck joined her back, the line where tanned skin faded to white.

She looked vulnerable, somehow. Fragile.

Fragile? Bradshaw?

Irritated, he turned to scan the jungle. The place was getting to him. They'd frightened away the birds, and now the butterflies that had swarmed above that clump of orchids had disappeared. The faint breeze that had trailed them here had vanished, as well, leaving the jungle around them still and silent, waiting for the impending rain.

Blame his edginess on the weather, then. It sure as hell wasn't making his job any easier. In a place like this, rain meant a downpour you'd damn near drown in. Nothing short of a solid roof would keep you dry, and there wasn't a roof within miles, solid or otherwise. Worse, getting drenched after heavy physical exertion guaranteed a good chill, even in this jungle heat. Five minutes after that he'd be sweating like a pig in the steam bath that inevitably followed a downpour.

At least it would wash away their tracks.

He glanced at the prints they'd made. Inexorably, one by one, they drew his gaze back to Bradshaw.

She was capping the last bottle when her head suddenly snapped up, her attention caught by something beyond the clearing.

"What do you hear?" Derrick demanded, instantly on the alert.

"Macaques. Monkeys. Something's spooked them."

Derrick caught it a second later—the angry, panicked hooting of a troop moving fast through the jungle behind them. "What set 'em off?"

"Could be any number of things." She calmly got to her feet. "Around here, however, the major four-legged predators are mostly nocturnal."

"Which leaves the two-legged kind. Great." He spun on his heel, scanning the jungle wall that encircled them. Amazing how fast paradise could turn into a trap. "I'm assuming they'll have spotted our tracks."

"Probably." Only the tilt of her head as she strained to hear betrayed the tension thrumming in her.

"Any other way out of this place?"

"No. No easy one, anyway. And we don't have the time to scale that rock wall. Besides, if they've already seen our tracks…"

Derrick nodded. "Then they might as well see us, too." He was already unfastening the buckles on his pack. He didn't want to look threatening, but he wanted plenty of freedom to move if he had to. "What's the chance they're friendly?"

That brought a humorless laugh. "You're joking, right? Though I do make a point of being *very* polite to the drug growers. Especially since several of them are old friends from the village."

"Always good to be on friendly terms with the neighbors." He'd rid himself of the pack and propped his rifle against it. Easy to grab if he had to, not so obvious it would be seen as an immediate threat. He hoped.

It all depended on who was headed this way. A hunter, even a poacher, wouldn't be too upset at finding strangers around, especially if they already knew Bradshaw. Given her past, chances were good that whoever was coming this way would at least know of her, even if they didn't know her personally, and would know she was a friend, not a threat.

But if it was drug traffickers, his and Bradshaw's mere presence on the trail could be seen as a very real threat, even if they were her friends.

On Pilenau, drugs meant marijuana, which flourished here in the heat and the tropical rains. It wasn't as profitable as cocaine or heroin, but for little more than the effort of harvesting it and hauling it out, a few hundred pounds of marijuana would provide a poor man with more money than he'd make in a year of honest labor. Enough to be worth killing for.

And they would kill. On Pilenau, a conviction for trafficking meant a life sentence in a prison in which average life expectancy could be measured in months, not years. That, or a short walk to face a firing squad. It was the sort of thing guaranteed to make a drug grower inclined to shoot first and toss the bodies in the jungle after.

It also guaranteed they'd want to know exactly whose footprints they'd found on any trails near their fields. He and Bradshaw could make a run for it, but that only meant that any confrontation would be on the other guys' terms, not his.

If it came to a fight, he preferred to set the terms himself.

"We want to look casual," he said. "Friendly."

"Too late for you, then," she snapped, clearly annoyed. "But I can start the teapot brewing if you like," she added sweetly.

"So how do *you* handle these situations?" he demanded, equally annoyed. Annoyed was better than guilty any day, and since he was the one who'd dragged her here… "Don't tell me you never run into anyone when you're out here on your own."

"I make a point of staying off the main trails and away from anywhere the Sword's operating. Or the drug growers. But then, I'm not usually traveling with a gun at my back."

She might have said more, but something on the trail behind them caught her attention. She held up her hand in silent warning. Derrick caught it a moment later—the faint sound of footsteps on wet, rocky ground.

"So," she said lightly and just a little more loudly than necessary. "You want tea? Or coffee?"

She moved away from him, but didn't set down her rifle. "Hello?" she called. Then a greeting in what Derrick supposed was Pilenauan.

The footsteps halted. A moment's silence, then an answering call, also in Pilenauan. The only thing Derrick understood in her response was "Dr. Lizzie."

The footsteps started again, moving a little more boldly this time. A moment later, two local men, each carrying an old rifle ready in his hands and a deadly *parang* at his waist, walked cautiously around that big mango tree and into the clearing. Two. And how many more out of sight behind the trees? Derrick wondered. He made no move toward his own rifle and kept his hands open at his sides.

Bradshaw smiled in greeting, then gave a little bow. She hadn't put down her rifle.

The man who seemed to be the leader hesitated, studying Derrick suspiciously, then cautiously bowed in return. "Dr. Lizzie," he said in heavily accented English. He didn't blink, and he didn't take his eyes off Derrick.

"Birat. And…Joseph Parman, right?"

The second man, clearly taking his cue from the one Bradshaw had addressed as Birat, nodded stiffly in acknowledgment. He hadn't taken his eyes off Derrick, either.

"This," said Bradshaw with a nod, "is Dr. Marx." She hadn't taken her eyes off the two men or her hands off her own rifle.

Nothing like a little staring match over rifles to set the tone for a discussion, Derrick thought sourly. He felt naked without his, but it was close enough. The other two hadn't missed the fact that it was within reach if they started something.

"Is doctor like you, Dr. Lizzie?" Birat asked, frowning at the machete in its loop on Derrick's belt and the multiple pockets on his clothes that could, and did, hide a number of weapons. No fool, this Birat.

"Sort of. He's interested in…butterflies," she said, deliberately provoking, then added an explanation in Pilenauan. Birat didn't look convinced in either language.

"We just finished filling our water bottles," she added. "Would you care to share some tea with us?"

Derrick choked back an instinctive objection. He didn't like it, but he had to let her play this her way.

"And maybe your friend behind you would like some, too?" she added with a friendly smile.

"Friend?"

"On the trail," she said, then repeated it in Pilenauan.

Birat wavered, clearly unhappy that his secret wasn't a secret at all. The man beside him looked even more unhappy, but when Birat lowered his rifle, then called out something in Pilenauan, he reluctantly lowered his rifle, as well.

A moment later, a third man nervously sidled out from behind the mango tree, rifle at the ready. Only a sharp command from Birat convinced him to lower the weapon.

Bradshaw's friendly greeting in Pilenauan didn't appear to reassure him any. Of the three, this one was the greatest threat because he was the most frightened.

Derrick gave him what he hoped was a friendly smile. The man flinched, hastily looked away.

Not good.

"So…tea?" Bradshaw beamed on everyone, the perfect hostess, delighted with her guests. She hadn't put her rifle down, either.

At Birat's curt nod of agreement, she bent toward her pack.

As though she'd flung a firecracker at his feet, the third man jumped back with a terrified squeak. He stumbled, righted himself and started jabbering in rapid-fire Pilenauan, rifle waving wildly between Derrick and her.

The sight of the gun that had magically appeared in Derrick's hand—the gun that was now pointed squarely between his eyes—simply made him back up faster, still jabbering in panic.

He only stopped when he realized that Bradshaw and the other two had only needed a few fractions of a second longer to get their weapons up, too.

"Bradshaw," Derrick said levelly, "I'd appreciate it if you'd tell your friends that this really isn't a good idea. You might also want to point out that there's more of them, but we've got better weapons."

Her equally rapid-fire Pilenauan made the other three glance nervously at their weapons. The second man shifted uncomfortably on his feet, but not one of the three lowered their rifles.

Birat, over a weapon pointed straight at Derrick's heart, studied the two of them. From the expression on his face, he wasn't happy about this little standoff, either. He was also clearly aware that the man behind him was as much of a danger to him and the second man as he was to them. Maybe more.

"You not doctor," he said accusingly.

"No," Derrick agreed. "But I'm not a threat to you, either. Not unless you force me."

Birat's grip on his weapon tightened. "You spy. You and Dr. Lizzie."

"I'm not a spy." Derrick didn't take his eyes off the

third man, who didn't seem at all reassured by a conversation in a language he couldn't understand.

"You *spy*," Birat insisted. "No one come here now.
Not with Sword close."

"He's telling the truth," Bradshaw assured him. "If I
were a spy, I would have reported your fields months ago."

That shook him.

"What fields you talk about?" he huffed.

She repeated it in Pilenauan.

That shook the other two.

She lowered her rifle but kept on talking, not giving
them a chance to argue. Derrick couldn't make out a
word she said, but he had no trouble telling when the
three men's defenses began to crumble. Birat was the
first to lower his weapon, but he didn't look happy about
it. Derrick waited until the other two started to relax
before he very slowly lowered his gun.

It took a sharp order from Birat for the idiot who had
started it all to finally put his rifle down.

Birat eyed him narrowly. "This true? You go find
brother? Brother with Sword?"

Derrick glared at Bradshaw. "What in hell'd you tell
him?"

She shrugged, unimpressed. "Enough. I had to. He
wouldn't have believed me, otherwise."

"Shit." He turned back to Birat, careful to keep his
expression neutral. "It's true. I have a brother who's
been…kidnapped by the Sword. I've hired Dr. Brad—
Dr. Lizzie to get me to the Ipona. That's all. We're not
interested in anything else. I don't want you telling

people about me any more than you want me telling people about you."

He wasn't sure how much of that Birat understood, but the native clearly grasped the essentials.

The man gave a sour smile, then spat on the ground at Derrick's feet. "No tell. No worry you tell. You dead man."

He barked an order that had his men reluctantly backing up, then turned back to Bradshaw.

"You go now, Dr. Lizzie. You not come back and you not tell, yes?"

"No, I won't come back, and I promise I won't tell. You know I won't. I never have."

Whatever she added in Pilenauan seemed to clinch the matter, because when she bent to gather up the water bottles that still stood on the rock at the water's edge, the three men simply watched, their gazes swinging warily between the two of them, but their rifles pointed down at their sides.

"Grab your pack, Marx," she said as she fastened the last buckles on hers. "I've got your water. We'll get it straightened out later."

The frightened one jumped as Derrick cautiously reached for his rifle, but seemed at least a little reassured when he set it aside to pull on his pack.

Still, he felt a little happier when he had the thing back in his hands. Gentlemen's agreements like this one had a nasty tendency to fall apart at the last minute, with very messy results.

"You get across the stream first," Bradshaw instructed him. "All the way across. Once you're across, then you can watch my back."

"I don't—"

"Just do it, Marx!" The bite in her voice was the first hint she'd given of just how on edge she really was.

Besides, she was right. As much as he hated being the first to walk away, the three would be less threatened by her than by him.

Which didn't mean he turned his back on any of them, not even crossing the stream. He stopped at the point where the trail disappeared into the jungle on the other side. "Your turn."

She bowed to the three men as calmly as if she were taking her leave after a pleasant chat over tea and cookies, then deliberately turned her back on them and came across the stream toward him.

Only once she was past him and was out of sight of the men in the clearing did Derrick follow.

She didn't look around when he caught up to her and didn't once glance back over her shoulder to be sure they weren't being followed.

"You trust them?" he demanded. "You sure they're going to just let us walk away like this?"

"No, but it's better than all the other alternatives."

He glanced over his shoulder. No one. The trail had taken a bend and now all he could see was more of that damned jungle closing in behind them.

He turned back to the trail ahead. It didn't look any more promising.

His heart was pounding so hard he was surprised Bradshaw couldn't hear it.

He couldn't help noticing that she had a stranglehold on her rifle. To stop the trembling in her hands, probably. That and the rapid rise and fall of her chest as her breathing tried to settle back to normal were the only signs that she'd been frightened back there in that clearing.

"I'm going to find a hiding spot and watch our back trail," he said. "I want to make sure they don't try to follow us. You go ahead and pick out a camp spot. A nice, *safe* camp spot. One where your friends aren't likely to come calling."

She glanced at him angrily. "Aren't you afraid I'll just leave you? Or maybe even circle back and shoot you myself?"

Derrick flinched. He deserved her anger and more, but now wasn't the time to tell her the truth. He still needed her, whether he liked it or not.

"I don't think you'll try it. Not until you're sure your little friend is safe, anyway."

With a choked cry of rage, she suddenly spun on him, fist clenched.

Derrick ducked. She swung again, aiming for his head, hitting his shoulder instead. It was a glancing blow, but it still hurt.

"Bastard! Birat was my *friend,* damn you! I've known him since I was a kid!"

When she swung a third time, he grabbed her wrist, pulled her against him, off balance and too close to cause much damage.

"He's growing drugs! You knew it! You admitted you knew it!"

"I guessed. It's not the same thing. And he wouldn't have threatened us at all if he weren't afraid of what the government would do to him if they ever found out."

Tears glittered in eyes narrowed by fury. The words were coming out in gasps, as if every syllable were painful.

"I've deliberately stayed away from this area. I've never told anyone, never said anything, and now, because of you—"

The words ended on a choked cry of grief and anger and the residue of real fear.

When she wrenched free of him, Derrick didn't try to stop her. She shoved him away, making him stagger.

"Go to hell, Marx. Just go to hell!"

And then she turned around and stalked off, away from him, as fast as her long legs would carry her.

She was almost out of sight when she stopped suddenly and spun back. "I'll make a camp, Marx, but I sure as hell won't make it easy for you—or them!— to find it!"

Chapter 5

Elizabeth wasn't sure how far she got before her shaky legs gave out under her. She sagged to the ground, head spinning, heart pounding like a mad thing. When the fear still churning in her belly threatened to come back up, she gritted her teeth and fought against the nausea.

Just what in hell had she gotten into? She was used to being afraid, but she wasn't used to what Marx did to her just by being close.

With a little moan, she slumped to sit with her back against a tree.

She'd been terrified, there at the clearing, and she'd truly been furious afterward, when the implications of what had happened finally hit. But it wasn't the danger, nor even the loss of an old friendship, that troubled her the most.

It was Marx, damn him. It was all Marx.

There at the stream, she'd felt him watching her. Not as prey senses a predator, but as a female senses a potent male. She couldn't help it. Maybe she'd been alone too long, but ever since he'd tended to her hand, ever since she'd felt the slide of his fingers across her skin and along the back of her leg, she'd been fighting against her own instinctive reaction to him.

It would have been easier to ignore if she still believed he might harm Niang. She didn't.

Not that the call to that Bear fellow hadn't been a nice bit of theater. But in the hours since she'd handed back the phone, she'd had time to think, time to watch and learn. She'd figured out a few things.

Like that bit about what Niang was wearing. At the time it had seemed to prove they really were watching the boy, that they were prepared to use him as leverage against her if she refused to cooperate. But the threat, and her belief in it, hinged on nothing more than a description of a shirt the boy was so attached to that it had become a joke in his village.

One of the supposed contacts that had led Marx to her could easily have dropped some casual comment about her "mail boy" and his fondness for that stupid T-shirt. After all, Marx was an American with money, money he was more than willing to spend to get what he wanted. What better way to convince him you knew what you were talking about—and ensure you got your share of his largesse—than to share a bit of casual, intimate trivia like that?

And she'd been the one who'd pointed out that the secret to getting your way was convincing your opponent you really would do what you threatened to do. She'd never said anything about actually *doing* it. If they'd hurt Niang—or convinced her they had—they'd have lost the only leverage they had over her. Marx knew that as well as she did.

Derrick Marx might be ruthless when it came to getting what he wanted, but he wasn't stupid. More important, he wasn't cruel. For Marx, the role of big brother was more than a trick of birth order. The man was instinctively protective, the kind of person who'd willingly put himself at risk before he'd ever allow anyone else to be harmed.

Which didn't mean he wouldn't use others if it suited his purposes. It didn't mean he wouldn't lie or cheat to get what he wanted. But Derrick Marx wasn't a threat to Niang and never had been.

But he was still a threat to her. Just not the kind of threat he'd intended.

And that left her….

Elizabeth grimaced. That left her sitting in the mud at the side of an elephant trail deep in the Pilenau jungle, wet, dirty, hungry and tired. Hard to imagine a less appealing combination.

Stifling a groan, she forced herself up. Once she was sure her legs had steadied enough to carry her, she set off down the trail. Marx could damn well catch up on his own.

He caught up just as she was kicking aside a downed tree limb to make room for her tent at one corner of the campsite. She'd already started a fire and had a small pot of water boiling to cook the rice and dried fish and vegetables that were her usual fare on the trail.

She glanced up, shoulders tensing, as he stepped out

of the bushes. She'd played this encounter a dozen different ways in her head over the past hour, but she still wasn't sure what to expect. She wasn't even sure what *she* would do, how she would react. Nothing in that lean-jawed face gave a hint as to what the man himself was thinking.

His impassive gaze swept across her crude camp, lingering on the fire, the cooking tools laid out on a broad leaf she'd picked, on the ground she'd already cleared. His gaze swung back to her, held.

Even across the empty space between them, she could *feel* him. The back of her injured hand tingled as if he still held it cradled in his.

Elizabeth bit back the angry, defensive words that trembled on her tongue. Let him make the first move.

She straightened, prepared for a fight if it came to that. A fight would be good. She wasn't much good at fighting, had never had much opportunity to practice, not even with Aaron when their marriage was disintegrating around them. But better a fight than trying to cope with her own confusing, unfamiliar reactions to this man who had almost cost her her life.

Seven steps divided them. She counted every one of them.

He stopped in front of her. There was at least a two-days' growth of beard on his chin. She had the oddest urge to brush a fingertip along that hard jaw, to feel the rough stubble against her skin. It had been so long, so very, very long, since she'd last touched a man like that.

She drew in a sharp breath. Her spine stiffened and her chin came up. A fight would be so...*safe*.

"Thanks," he said. "For everything."

She blinked. "What?"

He'd already turned away, as if he'd said all that needed to be said and had decided to move on to the next item on his agenda. He shed his rifle and pack, stretching his back with the air of a man glad to be rid of the load he'd been carrying, then bent over the bubbling pot to check its contents.

"Smells good. Is there enough for two?"

"Depends on how much you eat," Elizabeth shot back stiffly.

He glanced at her over his shoulder. The corner of his mouth crooked upward in a wry grin. "I eat a lot."

Her hands balled into fists at her side. After all they'd just gone through, he wanted to talk about *food?* "Then there's probably not enough."

"I've got MREs," he said, referring to the meals ready to eat. "And chocolate."

Saliva flooded Elizabeth's mouth. It had been a long time since she'd had chocolate. She swallowed. "What kind of chocolate?"

"Dark chocolate. Specially made for the trail."

"I only like really good Belgian chocolate."

Marx shrugged. "Place like this, you take what you can get, right?" He turned back to the fire. "That's an awfully smoky fire."

Damn the man! She wanted a fight, but on *her* terms, not his.

"If anyone's close enough to smell it, they're already too close," Elizabeth informed him. "Personally, I'd rather take my chances with hostile humans than with the mosquitoes."

"If you need bug spray—"

"I don't."

"Well, then…" He surveyed the narrow clearing again. "Where do you want your tent set up?"

"I can set up my own tent."

A muscle jumped at the side of his jaw. Good! It proved he wasn't impervious to her.

He drew a deep breath, let it out. "All right. Where do you want me to set up *my* kit?"

Elizabeth pointed to the rocky ground at the far side of the fire. "If you cut some vines and branches to lie on, you might not end up totally crippled in the morning."

"Thanks," he said dryly, and went to hack a hole in the jungle.

His "kit" was a waterproof sheet pegged over a rope stretched between a tree limb and a bush. It wouldn't do much to keep the rain off, but his comfort wasn't her concern.

In comparison, Elizabeth's own much-mended two-man tent was the Taj Mahal. Before spreading out her foam camp pad and blanket, however, she used its privacy for a rough washup and a change into dry clothes. If she'd been alone, she'd simply have walked out naked into the rain when it came, soap and shampoo in hand.

Yet another thing to hold against Marx, she decided,

grimly prodding her injured knee. She re-cleaned her scraped palm and knee, tucked her discarded garments under the tent's aluminum support poles to dry as best they could, combed her hair and retied it in her usual ponytail, then rolled out the camp pad and laid out her blanket.

The familiar routine was calming, but not calming enough for her to forget that Marx was there on the other side of that drawn tent flap. The thin nylon couldn't block out the sound of his footsteps or the distorted shadow he cast across the side of her tent every time he stepped between it and the fire. It was like watching a performance of the traditional Pilenauan shadow puppets, but without the usual narrator to tell the audience who the hero was and how he was going to win in the end.

They ate their dinner from leaf plates, silently scooping up the spicy fish and rice mix with their fingers while sitting cross-legged on the ground on either side of the fire.

Elizabeth kept her head down. Hungry as she was, her attention wasn't on the food.

Even without looking up, she followed Marx's every movement. The easy way he sat, the way his big hand cupped the leaf plate, the way his fingers curled as he lifted his bite to his mouth.

His mouth…

She'd been thinking about that mouth. About the way that hard line of lip could curl upward in a smile that startled with its warmth. She'd been thinking about the angles of cheek and jaw, the stubble of beard and the way it would feel beneath her fingertips if she were to trace that line of cheek and jaw and lip.

It would have been easier to ignore him if she still believed he might harm Niang.

He finished his food first. "That was good. Thanks."

He balled up the rice-smeared leaf and tossed it in the fire, then watched as the flames consumed it. Elizabeth couldn't help looking up, couldn't help watching him.

In the light of the fire, his face looked harder, his expression more distant and dangerous. Even through the smoke rising between them she could see his eyes glittering in the shadows.

The firelight only hinted at the jungle that loomed in the darkness behind him. The darkness where her ghosts waited.

She pushed the thought away. This time of night was always the hardest, when weariness made the world beyond the firelight loom hollow and vast and her defenses against memory were too weak to hold. She ought to be grateful for the distraction Marx provided. Maybe if she thought of him, she'd be able to sleep without dreaming.

She looked up to find him watching her with an intensity that made her skin prickle.

On the other hand, maybe not.

Abruptly, he got to his feet and stalked to the opposite edge of the clearing. There was nothing there but night.

Balked of escape, he turned to pace the perimeter. He didn't even bother pretending to check for danger. The jungle that, a moment before, had seemed a looming threat, was now a wall that held them penned in the gold-red intimacy of the firelight.

She would have felt…*safer* alone in the dark.

The silence was suddenly, painfully awkward.

He cleared his throat. "You, uh…you spend a lot of time camping out like this?"

She shrugged. "Sometimes."

He still wasn't looking at her. "Must get…lonely."

Another shrug, this time to cover the stabbing pain of truth. He probably knew as much about loneliness as she did.

She'd often wondered what Shanna would have thought of camping in the jungle, of sitting around a campfire and eating her dinner off a leaf. Her daughter had loved exploring the woods of Massachusetts and had often demanded Elizabeth tell her stories about her own childhood on Pilenau.

Elizabeth, remembering her years in the jungle alone with her father, had tried to ensure her daughter enjoyed all the normal childhood experiences that she herself had never had. Games out of boxes instead of from rocks and leaves. Trips to the mall and the movies. Ice cream and hot dogs and birthday cakes with candles. She had reveled in such wonderfully new and mundane things as much, if not more, than her daughter had.

Shanna had loved to sing. Maybe, if she'd lived long enough, she'd have taught her own mother some of the songs that most little girls learned, songs other than the ones Elizabeth had had to teach herself from books and tapes so that she could sing them to her precious, innocent little girl.

An explosion of sparks from the fire yanked her back to the present. Marx had returned to throw another branch into the flames. From the haunted look in his eyes, she suspected a few ghosts had walked out of the night to keep him company, too.

"We'll make the Ipona early tomorrow," she said when she could bear the silence no longer.

"Good," he grunted. "The sooner the better." His voice sounded rough, as if he'd had to drag it back from somewhere else.

Suddenly angry, at herself, not him, she tossed her own leaf plate into the fire and stood. "I'm going to sleep. You can put out the fire."

She could feel his eyes following her until she ducked into the bushes. When she emerged a few minutes later, his gaze was fixed on the fire again. He didn't bother looking up when she slipped into her tent and tugged the door flap down.

Sleep, however, eluded her. She was too tired, too conscious of Marx, still out there, staring into the fire. If she rolled on her left side, she could see him through the slit of the door flap. If she rolled onto her right, his hunched shadow swayed across the inner wall of the tent only inches from her nose.

If she closed her eyes, the image of her daughter drifted before her, eyes wide with puzzled blame.

She opened her eyes and wearily turned back to her left once more.

Eventually, Marx killed the fire and retreated to his own makeshift shelter. Elizabeth waited, senses straining, until she was sure he was asleep. Rather than torture herself by lying awake with nothing to look at except darkness and damp socks, she slipped out of the tent to sit cross-legged before it, staring up at the empty black vault above her and trying desperately not to think at all.

A sound, soft and strangled, jerked Derrick out of sleep.

He lay still, scarcely breathing, waiting for the sound to come again.

Nothing, not even a rustle of leaves.

He picked up the rifle beside him and peered out. Still nothing.

He wasn't accustomed to being wakened by nothing.

The sound came again, a low moan as of a creature in pain. And it had come from the direction of Bradshaw's tent. It took a moment for him to make out the outline of her body, black against darker black.

What was she doing sitting in front of her tent at this time of night?

Silently, rifle in one hand, flashlight in the other, he slid out of his shelter.

"Bradshaw?" He kept his voice pitched low and gentle. "You all right?"

If she heard him, she gave no sign.

"I'm turning on my flashlight."

He was almost on top of her when he brought the beam of the flashlight up to her face. At the anguished expression on her face, he froze. "What the hell…?"

The shock of the light snapped her out of her trance. Quick as a cat, she twisted and reached behind her.

She was fast. He was faster. He dropped both rifle and flashlight and launched himself across the couple of feet that divided them, pinning her to the ground. His hand closed around her wrist an instant before she got her rifle up to shoot him.

"It's me, Bradshaw! Let go of the rifle. Don't shoot!"

Beneath him, she went rigid as a board. He'd dropped the flashlight so he couldn't see her face, but he didn't need to see her to know when awareness finally kicked in. She shifted under him, relaxing back against the hard ground.

No, not relaxing. Sagging. The fear that had galvanized her into action had vanished just as quickly as it had come, leaving her limp.

"Marx?" Her voice sounded small and unsure.

"Yeah. It's me." He loosened his grip on her wrist but made no move to roll off her. "You want to let go of the rifle?"

Her fingers opened. The rifle hit the ground with a thump.

"I didn't hear you." The words were little more than a whisper. "I was listening, but I didn't hear…anything."

"Lady, I don't know what you were listening for, but it sure as hell wasn't me."

His own voice was raw-edged. The shock of what he'd seen in the flashlight's beam had shaken him more than he cared to admit.

He shoved her rifle away, out of reach.

"I'm letting you up now, okay?" He eased off her cautiously. She didn't move.

Derrick swore, then leaned forward and touched her face. Her skin was cold and clammy.

"Bradshaw? Elizabeth?"

She flinched, then abruptly rolled away from him and sat up. The abandoned flashlight cast enough light for him to see her hand shake as she dragged it through her hair.

"I'm all right," she said. Her voice shook, too. "You startled me, that's all."

"That's *all?*" He rocked back on his heels. "I saw your face, Bradshaw. I don't know where you went, but you sure as hell weren't here. What were you staring at? Ghosts?"

Instead of rousing her anger as he'd hoped, his harshness drove her back into herself. She drew up her legs and wrapped her arms around them, holding tight. Her shoulders hunched as she dropped her chin atop her knees.

He started to reach for her, then thought better of it and withdrew his hand.

"Bradshaw?" he prodded gently when she still hadn't answered.

"A lot of people see ghosts in the jungle. Nothing strange in that."

"But they don't sit up in the dark to watch them." She wasn't listening. The defensive walls she kept around herself were back up, higher and harder than ever.

"It's late and I'm tired." Without another word, she crawled into her tent, stretched out beside the rifle he'd forced her to drop, then pulled her blanket up over her head, effectively shutting him out.

All Derrick could see of her was the shadowy bulk of her body and the soles of her stocking feet. The sight roused the strangest urge to tuck her into bed like a weary child, draw up the covers and smooth the pillow, then turn out the light and silently tiptoe away.

Which was all the proof he needed that the jungle and Bradshaw were getting to him a hell of a lot more than he'd realized.

Chapter 6

The rain woke her. It hammered on the tent with deafening force, dragging her out of dark, unsettling dreams. Groggy and disoriented, Elizabeth blinked into the darkness, forcing herself awake. Goose bumps pricked at the night air's rainy coolness.

Nothing else had changed. Her rifle was reassuringly solid beneath her hand. Her pack made a familiar lump at her head. The camp pad beneath her was dry despite the deluge. Everything was as it should be, yet something didn't seem quite right.

Cautiously, she eased up on one elbow to peer out the far end of the tent and almost cried out in alarm at the massive black shape that blocked the opening.

Memory flooded in. And on the tail of memory, shame, then anger.

She sat up abruptly. A damp sock brushed against her nose. She batted it away.

"Marx? What in the devil are you doing sitting out in the rain like that?"

He shifted to look in the tent, a faceless, formless

bulk under the hooded waterproof poncho he wore. "You all right?"

"Yes, of course I'm all right. Why wouldn't I be?" The sock flopped wetly against her cheek.

"Sounded like you were having some bad dreams there."

Annoyed, she tugged the sock off the line and tossed it in the corner by her pack.

"I don't care about dreams," she lied. She had to raise her voice to be heard above the pounding of the rain. "And you haven't answered my question. Why are you sitting out in the rain like that?"

"Keeping watch."

As it often did in the jungle, the rain was coming straight down in sheets, and Marx was almost shouting to make himself heard over its pounding roar.

"In a downpour like this?"

"A tree limb came down across my tarp."

Maybe. But that didn't explain why he was standing guard against her dark dreams.

"Go back to sleep," he added curtly. "You'll need your strength tomorrow."

"So will you." She hesitated, but the solution was too obvious to ignore. "There's room for two in here if we stretch out on our sides. Dump your poncho and get in here before you drown."

"I don't—"

"Just *do* it, will you? Before I come to my senses and say to hell with good intentions."

Maybe he was just too tired and wet to argue, but

with a sigh that might have been relief, he slipped out of his poncho and into the tent.

It was a two-man tent, but Marx was a big man. He tried to keep as much distance as possible between them as he awkwardly worked his way under the tent, then stretched out beside her, but he still took up a lot of space. Worse, he and his abandoned poncho both dripped.

He bumped her foot. "Sorry."

"No problem." A burst of heat jolted her. In these dark, cramped quarters, it was inevitable he'd touch her, she reminded herself. *Inevitable.*

Despite the continuing roar of the deluge outside, she heard the rustle of his clothes scraping against the nylon ground sheet, his small, frustrated grunts as he tried to shift position without touching her. She wondered if he could hear the way her heart was pounding.

His knee touched the back of her thigh and as quickly withdrew. Heat flashed up her leg, making her flinch.

His hand brushed the curve of her back, her ribs. He jerked, tried to draw back and hit the side of the tent instead, setting the entire structure shaking.

Elizabeth shoved to her elbow, trying to give him more room. "Knock my tent down and you can sleep in the rain, Marx," she growled.

"Damn! Sorry." That was for his hand on her hip, instantly removed.

Something deep within her twisted, then flared hot. *Breathe,* she told herself, and sucked in air.

Beneath the sturdy cloth of her khakis, her skin

burned. The ghosts that had haunted her earlier, that had brought him to her, were forgotten.

It didn't matter much that she couldn't see him because she could feel and hear him. She could *smell* him. After a hard day's travel, he stank worse than she did.

But with the human stink was the scent of wood smoke and rain, dark, sweet, and delicately sensual.

Despite his wet clothes, the heat of their two bodies was already warming up the air around her, driving out the chill that seemed to go to her very bones.

"You're wet," she growled, retreating into the safety of irritation.

"Yeah. That happens when you stand out in the rain."

Even blinded by the dark, she could picture the way his mouth would have curved in a wry, slightly mocking smile as he said that.

He shifted again, trying, and failing, to give her more room. Evidently resigned, he settled onto his side behind her.

"Sorry for crowding you like this."

"It's all right." It wasn't.

She drew in a steadying breath, acutely conscious of how close he was, his legs spooned behind her legs, his hips a wall against hers.

Beneath the damp clothes, he was so *warm*. The skin of her back, her hips, her legs burned, as though his heat had set her body alight.

When his hand brushed her shoulder, she jumped.

"Take it easy, Bradshaw. I may stink, but I swear I won't bite."

"I didn't—"

"Lift your head up."

She would have refused, but her head had already come up from surprise. He slipped his arm under her. "Now lie down."

"I don't—"

He cupped his hand at the side of her head and pushed her down. "Relax."

Not with you this close! she wanted to snap. Somehow, her tongue couldn't quite wrap itself around the words.

Beneath her cheek his sleeve was rough and smelled of earth and man. Beneath the sleeve his arm was strong and solid and warm. Comforting.

She felt…*safe,* as if the sheer bulk of him was a sufficient bulwark against the world outside the tent and the dark dreams within.

Without thinking, she rolled her head a little, settling more comfortably against him. The movement pressed her back even closer against his chest.

The hand he'd cupped against her head slid down her throat, over her shoulder, down her arm. Her skin tingled at the friction of his palm even through the protective cloth of her shirt. The hand stopped. His fingers wrapped around her upper arm, then gently dug into the muscle, kneading it.

She almost jerked away, out of his arms, but his other forearm curled across her chest, holding her pinned against him.

"God, Bradshaw! These muscles get any tighter and they'll snap."

"I— Oh!" His fingers dug deep, finding the soreness close against the bone. He worked his way up the length of her upper arm, elbow to shoulder, then back again, probing, squeezing, stroking the stiffness she didn't know was there.

"Oh…" she breathed, more softly this time. It was almost a moan of pleasure. Almost.

His breath was warm against her ear, steady and even. His fingers were working magic on her tired body.

"That feels so…good," she said. It was barely a whisper.

"Yes." The single word caressed her cheek. His voice was husky, a little rough around the edges, and it sent butterflies zinging along her nerve endings.

She should move, shove him away and out of her tent. It was the safe, sensible thing to do. She couldn't budge. Her muscles refused to obey and her will was melting. The warmth rising in her belly and spreading through her chest and limbs was like syrup, thick and buttery sweet, infinitely soothing after a long and brutal day.

"Mmmm…." Her involuntary hum of pleasure vibrated at the back of her throat.

When he folded his arm across her chest so he could reach her other shoulder, she didn't even murmur a protest, just closed her eyes and curled closer against him, letting him work his magic.

"I'll keep you safe, Bradshaw," he said softly. His breath was warm against the back of her neck. Intimate. "I swear."

"I…" Her voice trailed off as her sleepy brain refused to respond.

"Go to sleep," he said, more softly still. "Go to sleep."

She would have argued the point, but a yawn caught her, swallowing any objections. Besides, she was warm now, and tired and, for a while at least, she was safe.

She shifted slightly, burrowing into the cave his arms had made around her. He said he would keep her safe and somehow she believed him.

Strangely comforted, she drifted into dreamless sleep.

Derrick drifted up out of sleep regretfully. Then he remembered where he was, and why.

For a moment he considered simply going back to sleep, close and warm against the still sleeping Bradshaw. But only for a moment. He didn't dare indulge his fantasies any longer than that. The dull gray light said dawn wasn't far away. They had to be on the trail by then.

He knew the instant Bradshaw awoke. She came awake slowly. Her breathing deepened, then she stirred, stretching a little, and nuzzled his sleeve. His arm and shoulder were stiff from having been in one position so long, but he didn't attempt to ease the cramp. Let her wake on her own. She'd pull away from him soon enough, in more ways than one. The thought brought a vague feeling of regret.

He ignored the feeling, then stifled a groan as she rolled, then stretched again, a movement which brought her back flat against his chest and her hips firmly into his lap.

A man has his limits, Derrick thought, and he'd just

reached his. With his free hand, he gave her shoulder a shake. "Bradshaw? Bradshaw! Wake up!"

"Hummm?" Her hand flopped weakly. She might have been brushing off an annoying fly. "G'way."

She sighed, then curled into a ball with a burrowing motion as if settling into a fat feather pillow.

Derrick gritted his teeth and gave her another shake, harder this time. "Bradshaw!"

That brought her up with a jerk. Her hand was reaching for her rifle before her eyes were fully open.

He wrapped his free hand over hers just as her fingers curled around the stock. "It's me. Marx. It's okay."

The instant her grip on the rifle relaxed, he let go and rolled back, giving her room. She scrambled to a sitting position and scooted away, eyes wide, chest rising and falling in the rapid, shallow pattern of someone who'd been hit with an adrenaline punch.

He levered up to his elbow, wincing at the stabbing needles as feeling returned to his arm. "Sorry I startled you."

She blinked, breathed deeply, then dragged a shaking hand through her hair, which had tumbled free of her ponytail. "What time is it?"

"Close to dawn." He checked his watch. "Five-ten, to be exact."

"So late?" She glanced out the open end of the tent, still disoriented. "How can it be that late? I *never* sleep this late. Why didn't you wake me sooner?"

"We've got a hard morning ahead of us. You were entitled to a good night's sleep."

That made her blink. "A good night's sleep," she echoed wonderingly, as if that were something she didn't know much about.

He could tell the instant she remembered just *how* she'd slept, there beside him on the ground with her head pillowed on his arm. The sudden blush that swept her tanned cheeks startled him. Blushing wasn't something he'd have connected with the tough, practical Dr. E. B. Bradshaw, who slept with a rifle inches from her hand.

She looked good with her hair down, softer and less intimidating. Beautiful despite the bits of leaf tangled in those long dark locks or the smudge of dirt on her jaw. Sexy, too. She looked, in fact, like a woman who had just spent the night with a man.

Too bad all they'd done was sleep.

Rather than follow that line of thought, he grabbed his own rifle and backed out of her tent, then bent to help her up. She glanced at his outstretched hand as if she expected some trick. He thought she'd refuse his assistance, but then her hand slid into his. The feel of her warm, callous-roughened palm pressed against his hit with an electric jolt.

For an instant he had a vivid mental image of that slender, capable hand on *him*, bare skin against bare skin. Just for an instant, but that was enough. When he let go and stepped back, his own breathing had turned shallow and a little fast.

If his touch had affected her, she didn't show it. She flattened her hands on the base of her spine and arched backward, stretching like a cat. That wasn't any better for his breathing than her touch had been.

"Pack up," he said roughly. "There's no time for a fire or hot food. We'll eat on the trail. I have MREs for both of us."

"How nice," she said dryly. She straightened without hurry and glanced at the lowering cloud cover just beginning to be visible above them. She shot him a sour look. The wary prickliness of yesterday was back in spades. "MREs, no tea, more rain and *you.* What a lovely way to start the day."

He almost apologized but bit the words back in time. Last night had lowered barriers between them that should never have been breached. It was his problem that he'd come to want them totally demolished.

His things were quickly repacked. While she finished stowing her possessions, he pulled out the satellite phone.

"Bear, talk to me."

"About time you called, buddy," Bear growled from the other end of the line. "We've got problems."

"Damn. Damn, damn, damn, *damn.*"

Elizabeth couldn't have put it better herself.

From beneath the protective cover of a towering clump of bamboo, Marx glared at the swollen, muddy river swirling past his feet, then at the fat gray rain clouds that hung low over the slopes of the volcano above them.

"Must be raining like hell up there," he said.

"It's still passable." But just barely, she added silently to herself.

Frowning, she studied the river whose roiling surface

mirrored the emotions churning within her. The unfamiliar sense of safety, almost of peace, that Marx had brought her last night was gone, and the lack of it made the hollows within her seem even deeper and darker than before. In a few minutes Marx would be across the river and she'd still be here, alone.

A half-drowned log floated past, its twisted branches a child's hands, desperately reaching for her own outstretched hand. She shut her eyes, blocking out the sight. Her heart pounded.

It's a *log,* she told herself. A piece of deadwood, nothing more. She forced her eyes open.

The log slid past, tumbled over and disappeared beneath the river's surface.

Her chest was so tight, it hurt to breathe. *Breathe anyway.*

"The ford's there." She pointed. "See? Right there where the river widens out."

It was a log. *Just a damned, dead log.*

"How deep is it there?"

"On you, maybe waist high at the deepest. That's assuming you don't hit a hole on the way across."

"Shit! The 'experts' told me this river never got past your knees here."

"It doesn't. Unless it's been raining hard." Elizabeth forced a careless shrug. "There's one good thing—with the river like this, the crocs won't be much of a problem."

He glanced at her, startled. "They said there weren't any crocs."

"They lied."

He turned back to the river. "Great. Just…great."

Ever since they'd broken camp this morning he'd been angry, almost hostile, yet strangely remote. Whatever he'd learned in that phone call he'd made was not good news.

Didn't matter. It wasn't her problem. She'd done what he'd forced her to do, gotten him here as fast as humanly possible. She'd get him to the top of the ridge and from there he was on his own.

And so was she. *Alone. Again.* Just as she'd been ever since Shanna had died.

Elizabeth stared out across the angry Ipona, but she couldn't quite focus. The scene before her was overlaid with memories of another place half a world away.

The rain-swollen Massachusetts stream that had claimed her daughter's life hadn't been this wide or deep, but it had been rocky and angry and, when that muddy bank had collapsed, more than powerful enough to rip Shanna from her grip and carry her away forever.

"Where's this route up the cliff you promised me?"

Marx's harsh question dragged her back to the present. She swallowed the lump that had risen in her throat, blinked to clear her vision.

"See that vertical ridge above the bamboo?" she asked, pointing again. It was hard to get the words out. "The way up's behind there. You can't see it from here, but you shouldn't have any trouble finding it once you're on the other side."

He studied the ridge she indicated. "I won't have any trouble at all, since you're going to take me all the way up."

"What?" She spun to confront him. "No!"

"All the way up." His eyes were hard as stone.

"The hell I will! You said you wanted me to get you to the Ipona fast and show you the way up the ridge. Well, here you are, there's the way.... I'm not budging another inch."

He shook his head. "The army's moved up their rescue plans. Bear told me this morning. The main body of the Sword hit the port last night, almost twenty-four hours early. The army got most of them, but the ones they didn't are headed this way."

"Not my problem, Marx."

"I'm afraid I made it your problem, Bradshaw. Those drug runners yesterday…" Something flickered, deep in his eyes. "You said it yourself. Anything happens—like me being here, like you being spotted near the Ipona— everyone around here knows about it, sooner or later. Including the Sword."

"But I—"

"The locals may not have words for numbers greater than ten, Bradshaw, but they can add two and two just fine. If any of those terrorists slip out of the army's hands, they'll eventually be coming after *you*. You know it as well as I do."

Elizabeth's stomach went queasy. The Sword were infamous for the ruthless vengeance they wreaked on anyone who opposed them.

"In the meantime—" a muscle in Marx's jaw jumped "—I've only got a few hours left. I'm not going to waste them looking for the route on my own. You're taking me

up that cliff, and then you're going to take me as close
to the Sword's camp as you can get me. And then…"
He hesitated. "And then you're coming out with me
when Charley picks us up."

Panic struck. Leave Pilenau? She could feel her
throat seize up, just at the thought.

"Go to hell!"

"I'm sure I will," he said grimly. He stepped out of
the covering bamboo. "But I'm going up that cliff, and
so are you. Let's go, Bradshaw."

"No!" She tried to shove past him. He shifted into
her path. She planted her hands flat against his chest and
shoved. He didn't budge an inch.

"It's my brother's *life*, Bradshaw. Whatever crimes he's
committed, he doesn't deserve to die for them. Not here.
Not like this. Don't you see?" he added, openly pleading.
"If you don't help me now, you'll have to live with the
knowledge that you could have helped save a man's life,
but didn't. Do you really want to carry a burden like that?"

She stared up at him bleakly. "What's one more?"

"What?"

He was right, though. She didn't need another death
on her conscience.

"All right," she said, defeated. "You win." The secret
to survival, she'd learned, was to not think, to just keep
moving. So…she'd move.

The river hit her, hard, fast and cold. Ten feet from
the bank it was up to her hips and trying hard to drag
her under. Another ten feet and it was to her waist and
quickly getting deeper.

Inch by inch she fought her way forward. Marx was only a couple of feet behind her, but she couldn't see him without turning, couldn't hear him above the roaring of the river.

Don't think. Keep moving. Just. Keep. Moving.

The water was above her waist now. Every step was a battle she was beginning to think she couldn't win.

A stone, half-buried in the muddy river bottom, turned under her foot. She stumbled. The river slammed against her side, twisting her around so the weight of her rifle and pack tipped her even further off balance, threatening to pull her under.

For an instant, for the thousandth of a second that it took the thought to form, she considered simply letting go and letting the river take her. It would be so easy. Just quit fighting and give in. No more remembering, no more guilt or loss or grief.

The river would take her and that would be the end of it. There was justice in it, and peace, perhaps. Or at least oblivion.

Her knees buckled.

Almost, she let go. Her convulsive struggle to regain her footing was animal instinct, not rational thought.

Coward! the voice in her head shouted. *It isn't this easy. It wasn't meant to be this easy.*

And then hands, big, strong hands, grabbed hold of her and pulled her up.

Gasping, she sagged gratefully against Derrick Marx's chest while the river swept relentlessly past. Her heart hammered in her chest. Her legs quivered from the strain of staying upright. He stood like a rock, legs braced, his arms tight around her, holding her safe.

He bent his head, shouting against the rush of the river. "You okay?"

She nodded without raising her head. A buckle on his pack strap scraped her ear. The slight pain was wonderful, proof she was still alive.

"Let me carry your pack."

"No!" She tried, and failed, to pull free of his protective embrace. "I'm fine. I just slipped, that's all. And I'm almost halfway across, anyway."

Marx looked like he wanted to strangle her. "Don't be stupid!"

"I already was!" she shouted. "I don't intend to be stupid again." She shrugged to get her pack into balance, suddenly angry. At him, for saving her. At herself, for needing to be saved. "Move, would you, so I can get out of this damned river."

Head down, she took one cautious step, then another.

She'd slipped, that's all, she angrily told herself. She'd lost her footing and gotten caught by the current. There was nothing in it. Absolutely nothing at all.

Still, beneath the protective anger, there was profound relief that Derrick Marx was half a step behind her, ready to catch her and pull her back to safety if she slipped again.

Chapter 7

Derrick followed her across the river, cursing all the way. He cursed himself. He cursed the river. The weather. Her. The murderous fanatics who'd brought them here. His brother. *Her.* And then she walked out of the river and slumped down on a rock to catch her breath, and something deep within him twisted tight.

His heart had damned near stopped when she'd started to go under; then, when she'd clung to him, it had almost hammered its way out of his chest. And not just out of relief, dammit.

Focus, he told himself.

He tilted his head back to look at the seemingly vertical cliff towering above them. Even here, on the other side of the river, he couldn't see the way up that Bradshaw swore was there.

He glanced to where she now sat, calmly wringing out her socks. A dry pair sat atop an open plastic bag lying on the rock beside her.

She'd nearly drowned, and now she was changing her socks? Derrick shook his head, puzzled.

He'd have sworn there'd been something beneath her panic and subsequent anger, some emotion he couldn't quite name. Whatever it was, she'd drawn back behind that invisible wall she kept so tightly wrapped around her. She was as distant now as if she'd fled to another place, one far from him and the river beside them.

And what business was it of his, anyway? He'd threatened and manipulated her and lied to her. He'd deliberately dragged her into danger, and now he was forcing her closer still. Guilt, however, would have to wait, along with whatever else it was she stirred up in him.

He unbuckled his pack and let it slide to the ground. He was in the process of excavating the bulky weight at the bottom when she came to stand over him. Derrick glanced up. "Ready?"

"Are you?"

It sounded like a challenge, not a question. Bradshaw was back in fighting mode.

"Almost." He lifted out the bundle and set it aside, then rapidly repacked. "Find a good spot to hide that, would you? Someplace close to the river where we can get to it fast, but it can't be spotted from the air."

She nudged it suspiciously with the toe of her boot. "What is it?"

He stood, picked up his pack. "Inflatable raft."

"You said you were getting out by helicopter."

Derrick met her accusing glare straight on. "I am. But I like to have options."

She glanced at the river, then back at the raft. "You'd better hope you don't need them, Marx."

* * *

The guilt Derrick felt at having forced Bradshaw across the river with him died on the climb up the cliff.

She hadn't lied when she'd said he could have found the route on his own, but he would have wasted time he didn't have trying. The chute, almost invisible unless you were right in the middle of it, was filled with dirt and crumbling rock and choked with plants and young trees that had found a tenuous anchorage in the unstable ground. You could climb the thing, but he hoped to hell he didn't have to go back down it.

Despite the weight she carried and the battering she'd taken in the river, Bradshaw went up with the agility of a monkey. He was pretty sure she didn't deliberately cause the occasional falls of rocks and dirt that kept him watchful, but he wouldn't swear to it.

The only news Bear had had since that first morning call had been grim, grimmer and grimmer still. The Sword was scattered but traveling fast, trying to bury themselves in the jungle where it would be harder for the pursuing soldiers to find them.

So far as anyone knew, they hadn't yet been able to communicate with their camp, but that didn't rule out the possibility of some kind of dead man's code, say an order to kill all the hostages if the camp hadn't heard from the attack force by a certain time. Chances were good it hadn't gone that far—the Sword were murderous fanatics, not suicidal—but Derrick still worried. In this business, he'd long since learned, no news was almost always very bad news indeed.

A clatter of stone on stone made him look up, then swing to the side as a small avalanche of dirt and rock hurtled past.

Ten feet above him, Bradshaw was grimly hanging on to a tree root, trying to regain her footing, and swearing. He liked the sound of the swearing. Better that than the hollow, heart-pounding silence from back there in the middle of the river.

Don't think about her. He scowled at an unoffending weed in front of him. *Don't think about how you've thoroughly mucked up her life.*

Above him, Bradshaw was climbing again. She grabbed hold of a rock, paused, then glanced back down at him. "Coming, Marx?" she called mockingly. "Or did you think we had all day to do this?"

Derrick swore and started climbing.

When he finally scrambled over the top, he found Bradshaw sprawled in the shade of an overhanging tree, breathing hard. She glanced at him, then up at the sun just visible through the trees.

"You must have been born lucky, Marx. I'd have sworn we wouldn't make it this far, and certainly not this quickly."

He dropped, panting, beside her. "We made a good team, Bradshaw."

"Who said anything about a team?" She got to her feet.

The top of the cliff was as densely forested as every other inch of ground they'd covered so far, but there was no mistaking the faint trail that led from the cliff into the heart of all that green.

Bradshaw studied the ground, then the mass of undergrowth and vines.

"No sign of anyone through here recently," she said. "But then, there's no reason for the Sword to come this way."

"And the locals?"

"Hah! They're not crazy, Marx, even if you are." She settled her pack more comfortably, picked up her rifle. "We go this way."

Once again, her knowledge of the terrain made all the difference. Without ever consulting the map where she'd drawn in all the secret hidden pathways through her world, she led him along a faint trail that at times disappeared beneath the relentless growth but never quite vanished. Sooner than he'd expected, she halted and drew him aside, off the trail.

"That's your clearing for the pick up," she said. "But your pilot better be good if you expect him to land there."

"Charley's good." *He's going to have to be.*

Derrick studied the man-made clearing that was quickly being reclaimed by the jungle. At the far side, crumbling, palm-thatched huts marked the death of someone's dreams for a home and a future. But there was enough flat ground for Charley to put down, and that was all that mattered. That and being sure he was back with Danny in time.

He glanced at Bradshaw. She was studying the huts, her expression grim. "You know this place?"

"Friends built it," she said. Her voice sounded

distant, strained. "They're gone now. Or dead. The Sword drove them out."

A trickle of sweat slid down the side of her cheek, tangling with a lock of hair that had worked free of her ponytail.

He reached out and gently smoothed the lock back. That was a mistake.

Her eyelids were already sliding shut when he kissed her.

It was a short, hot, searing kiss. A kiss with fury in it, and need, a kiss with everything that lay between them that neither dared put into words, and every dangerous thing that lay ahead for which they needed no words at all.

Eventually he let her go and stepped back. For an endless moment her gaze locked with his.

"I'll be back," he said softly. "Soon." His hand rose to touch her, dropped. "Wait for me."

Then he turned and, without a backward glance, slipped into the jungle in the direction of the terrorists' camp.

Dazed, Elizabeth stared at the wall of jungle into which Marx had disappeared. In the trees above her, a bird called, a bulbul—*Cheer! Chip-cheer! Cheer!*— then fell silent. She couldn't see it, not even when a sudden flap of wings told her it had taken flight.

Now that Marx was gone, the bold, brash facade she'd donned like a cloak disappeared, leaving her feeling vulnerable and very much alone.

He had said to wait.

She needed to leave. Right now. She needed to get back down that cliff and across the river while she still could.

She pressed shaking fingers against her lips. Her feet refused to budge.

Even though the terrorists' camp was too far away, she strained for some sound, some hint of what was happening.

Nothing. Nothing but the jungle around her, familiar and unchanged.

And yet, because of Marx, everything had changed. He was right. If any of the Sword escaped, her life was at risk. She *had* to leave.

But could she?

The clearing in front of her was still empty and silent, but in her mind she saw a chopper hovering there, its engines roaring, its big rotors whipping the air as they fought to keep the thing balanced between earth and sky. She saw Marx in the open doorway, eyes hot and urgent, his hand outstretched, ready to snatch her out of her world and into his if only she could reach him.

She could see it so *clearly*. His face. The set of his jaw. That outstretched hand. And then the chopper lifting, rising higher and higher until it was just a speck on the horizon while the clearing fell silent behind it, as though no one had been there at all.

Elizabeth fought against rising panic. Her stomach churned. Her lungs felt as if some giant hand were squeezing them, cutting off her air.

She could see all that, but she couldn't see herself.

She couldn't see her hand in Marx's hand or her face in the open doorway as the jungle fell away beneath them.

She couldn't see herself because she wasn't there.

Trembling, she sank to her knees. The sweat that drenched her came not from heat but fear.

She'd avoided the truth for too long. After years of hiding from her pain in the heart of Pilenau, the outside world, the world that had taken her daughter from her, had become more terrifying than any terrors the island itself might hold.

Like her father before her, she had become a prisoner in a prison of her own making. She *couldn't* leave Pilenau, even if it cost her her life to stay.

From behind a screen of leaves Derrick studied the Sword's camp. A couple of long houses, each large enough to hold a dozen men, maybe more. The shabby camouflage pants and worn T-shirts draped over ropes strung between the houses gave the place an oddly domestic air.

In the open-walled mess hut at the center of the compound, four men sat hunched over a card game, their weapons forgotten. Derrick could see another three…four…five men. Two clearly on guard duty, one asleep in a hammock, the last seated at a crude work table cleaning his rifle.

And there, off to the side and almost invisible behind the crude bamboo palisade that surrounded them, stood four tiny huts. According to the informant, Danny was in the one on the right.

It took him fifteen minutes to work his way around the camp to the palisade. Silently, every sense on alert, he slipped out of the bushes, knife in hand.

The palisade wall looked solidly intimidating, but only a few of the bamboo poles had actually been set in the ground. Between the uprights the poles were lashed to each other with crude ropes made by men who weren't much interested in rope making. A little careful sawing with the knife and he swung up a section of bamboo and slipped through, then dropped the section back into place.

Once through, Derrick paused, studying the ground in front of him. From outside the palisade came the muted murmur of voices spiked by an occasional growl of disgust or crow of success from the gamblers.

There was no sound of helicopters, no hint that the quiet and routine would soon be shattered. How long did he have?

Feeling like there was a demon riding him, gnawing away at the little time he had left, he silently glided forward.

Elizabeth took the same path back to the river that she and Marx had taken such a short time before. Now that she was moving again and on her own in the jungle, the panic had retreated. It had left her shaken and ashamed, but she couldn't think about that now. She didn't dare let herself think about what might lie ahead, either.

Sufficient unto the day, her father had always said.

He'd been afraid to leave the jungle, too.

She had a dozen reasons why this really was the best course of action. After all, her work was here on Pilenau, not back in some university. It was normal to want to remain where you'd grown up. The army would win, the Sword would be broken and she wasn't at risk. Life would go on as it had before.

More important, she would forget she'd ever met Derrick Marx. She would forget that he'd lied to her and used her, that he'd dragged her into danger, then kissed her and told her to wait for him. She would forget what it had felt like to sleep without dreaming and wake with him curled comfortingly warm and strong against her.

Somehow, it didn't sound very convincing, but what did it matter? This time tomorrow, she'd be home.

Something in her chest squeezed painfully at the thought.

Not home. *Camp.* A couple of tents on wooden platforms, some battered cookware, a cot, a chair, a table…and her work. It was nothing like the home she'd once dreamed of. The home she'd almost had, for a little while.

One day at a time. That was the rule she'd set for herself after Shanna died. One day at a time. One hour if she couldn't face twenty-four of them. One step at a time if she couldn't manage anything else.

And don't look back!

That was the hardest rule of all.

It had all gone better than Derrick had expected. By the time he cautiously lifted the wooden latch to

Danny's cage, he was beginning to think he actually might make it. Then he saw the ragged, broken figure curled on the dirt floor of the airless prison.

His luck had just run out.

Heart pounding, he knelt beside his brother. "Danny?" No response. He gave his brother's shoulder a gentle shake. "Come on, buddy. Wake up. It's time to go."

Danny's eyelids fluttered, slid slowly open.

"Hey, guy," Derrick said softly. "It's me. Derrick."

"Der?" It was barely a whisper. Dan blinked, trying to focus. "Der? Is that really you?"

"It's really me, Dan." Derrick had to fight against the hot thickness in his own throat. "I've come to take you home."

For a moment, his brother just lay there staring up at him with the puzzled look of a man drifting out of a dream.

"Dan?"

Danny tried to speak, choked, screwed his eyes shut against the tears he couldn't stop. "I was so afraid you wouldn't come."

Derrick squeezed his brother's shoulder reassuringly. The depth of the trust behind those simple words cut more cruelly than any blame.

"Sorry it took so long," he said. "Somehow, I'll make it up to you, Danny, I swear. But right now we have to get you out of here. Come on."

He slid a hand under his brother's shoulders and started to lift him to a sitting position, but stopped at Danny's sharp hiss of pain. He gently laid him back down.

"So," he said lightly, fighting not to let his fear show. "A little banged up, are you?"

Danny's laugh broke on a ragged gasp. "A little," he admitted weakly. "Cracked head. Cracked rib. Busted ankle." For the first time, Derrick noticed the crude brace of sticks bound with tattered rags on his brother's left ankle.

"About the same as when you smashed up your cycle last June, then." Derrick gave his brother's shoulder a gentle punch. "Sounds like you'll live."

Bad joke. His brother's face crumpled.

"I thought I was going to die, Der. I thought they were going to kill me, just like they killed that other guy." He was choking on his tears. "I heard him screaming. He was begging them not to kill him but—"

"Dan."

His brother sank back weakly, blinking against the tears.

"No time for that now, buddy," Derrick said more gently. "We gotta get you out of here. Some friends are coming in with a chopper and we don't want to miss them."

"I can't walk, Der." Danny's voice had sunk to a hoarse whisper.

"Then I'll carry you. Whatever it takes."

Derrick helped his brother to his feet as gently as he could, but when he started to move, Danny pulled back.

"What about...the others?"

"Already gone."

"Gone?"

"Later," Derrick snapped. "I'll explain later. Right now, we're getting the hell out of here."

Teeth gritted against the pain, his too-thin face pale, yet set hard with determination, Danny managed better than Derrick had expected. Once through the palisade and into the jungle beyond, Derrick slipped his arm around his brother, taking some of Danny's weight, wishing he could take the pain.

Don't think about how thin he is, he warned himself. *Don't worry about what they've done to him.* They were getting out. That was what mattered now. Worry could come later.

They were halfway to the pickup point when Derrick heard the first cry of alarm from the terrorists' camp behind them.

At the sound Danny froze, then turned to look even though there was nothing to see behind them but green. "They know," he said. It was barely a whisper. "They've found out we're gone."

"Or the army's hit the camp," Derrick said grimly.

Danny swung back to stare at him. "You knew they were going to rescue us?"

"They're after the Sword, Danny. They want to rescue the hostages, too, but—" He hesitated, then added, "They know about the drugs, Dan."

The stricken look in his brother's eyes killed Derrick's last doubts. His brother really had been dealing drugs.

"Come on," he said. "Charley's not going to wait."

The sound of gunfire behind them added an extra note of urgency.

As they struggled along one of the almost invisible
trails that Bradshaw had told him would lead back to the
clearing, Derrick found himself worrying about her as
much as about his brother or the army. He'd told her to
wait, but his gut told him she'd be long gone by the time
he and Danny got there.

Something was holding her here in this damned
jungle. Not her work, but *something*. He'd seen it in her
eyes. Just the suggestion that she should leave with him
had been enough to make her panic.

The distant *whump-whump-whump* of helicopter
rotors, coming closer, brought his head up with a snap.
Charley? Or the Pilenau army?

Ignoring Danny's gasp of pain, he tightened his grip
on his brother and broke into a stumbling jog trot, half
dragging, half carrying his brother.

Through the screen of trees, Derrick caught the
gleam of light reflecting off the whirling rotors. The dull
black body of the chopper was like a shadow, half-
hidden by the intervening jungle.

Whump-whump-whump. Only this time the sound
wasn't from the clearing ahead, but from the sky behind.
Danny glanced up, face strained with fear, but Derrick
refused to take his eyes off that black shadow ahead.

A hundred yards. Eighty.

The vines across the path reached out to grab them,
trying to tangle their feet.

Faster. *Faster*.

Danny's breath was coming in a hard, gasping rattle.
Every step brought a choked moan of pain. With each

hopping, stumbling step he batted at the branches in their way, violent swings as if he were trying to lift up off his broken ankle and fly.

They almost made it.

Twenty yards left. That was all. Twenty jungle-choked yards.

It might as well have been a mile.

With a scream of engines pushed to the max, the chopper in the clearing lifted, tilted, then leapt into the air, setting the trees thrashing in the backwash.

They reached the edge of the clearing just in time to see the big black chopper clear the treetops. A moment later it was gone, the rapidly fading sound of its engines swallowed up in the roar of the approaching pursuers.

A heartbeat later, a chopper bearing the insignia of the Pilenau army sliced across the blue sky above them like a hungry hawk. Then a second appeared. But they, too, disappeared.

Derrick didn't have time even to curse. With a low moan, Danny fainted.

Chapter 8

The first helicopter, black and deadly, roared over the treetops perhaps a quarter of a mile from where Elizabeth crouched in the bushes at the top of the cliff. The pilot was either crazy or very, very good, because he didn't slow as he cleared the trees, dove toward the river, then banked to race north along the cliffside at what seemed a hair's breadth from disaster. He was going so fast he was out of sight before two more copters, both clearly marked with the insignia of the Pilenauan army, roared past in pursuit.

It seemed an eternity before she saw the army helicopters reappear above the trees, perhaps a mile or so upriver. They were moving more slowly now, and they were clearly headed back in the direction from which they'd come.

From her hiding place, Elizabeth let out the breath she didn't know she'd been holding. The pilot of the first chopper had gotten away, then. She would have heard if the army had brought him down.

Marx was on that first chopper. Marx and his brother. He had to be.

It was the possibility that he might not be, that he might not have reached the rendezvous in time, that had kept her here, hidden, waiting.

If he was forced to escape via the river, he'd need her help. That's what she'd told herself when she'd found she couldn't take that first step down the cliff.

It wasn't a lie. *If* he had his brother, *if* he came this way, he *would* need her.

And if he didn't come this way?

She had no way of knowing what had happened. The distant gunshots, the pursuing helicopters, all said she was a fool to wait.

Yet she couldn't get him out of her head. The grief and love and worry she'd seen in him when he spoke of his brother. His touch. His rare, twisted smile. The warmth and strength of his body against hers when the night was dark and cold and lonely. The rock-solid sureness with which he'd held her, there in the river, when her own pain would have swept her under.

So she was a fool. What else was new?

And because she was a fool, she waited.

She heard him long before she saw him. Heard *someone,* anyway. There was no mistaking the heavy footsteps of a two-legged man for the quicker, quieter tread of any four-legged creature that size. Whoever it was was coming fast and making no effort to be quiet.

Pursuers? she wondered. Or the pursued?

An instant later she had her answer when Marx stepped out of the jungle darkness into sun.

She wasn't even aware of her own movements. One

moment she was crouched deep in the cover of the undergrowth, the next she was standing on the path in front of him.

At the sight of her, Marx stopped short, breathing hard, clearly startled. He was dirty and dripping sweat and Elizabeth felt her heart lift as soon as she saw him.

Her gaze slid to the unconscious man draped over his shoulders.

"He's alive," she said. It was barely a whisper. "Your brother's alive. *You're* alive." She wanted to shout for the miracle she hadn't really believed in.

"What in hell are *you* doing *here?*" Marx demanded.

The fury in his voice snapped her head up. "Waiting for you."

"I told you to wait at the pickup point!"

Her temper flared. "Fat lot of good *that* would have done me. It certainly didn't work for you!"

"They put down. You could have gotten out even if we didn't."

"Yeah, with the Pilenau army hot on the trail." She bit back her anger and turned her attention back to the unconscious man draped over his shoulders. "We're wasting time arguing. Your friends are gone and we're still here. Put your brother down so I can take a look at him."

Marx swallowed whatever he'd been about to say and eased his brother to the ground.

"How bad?" she asked, kneeling.

"He'll live. He just passed out." Something in Marx's expression said he was trying to convince himself more than her.

"Better that way." She checked the makeshift splint, lifted the edges of the bandages on his arm and head. Danny's pulse was fast but strong, the breathing a little shallow, as if catching in pain. A broken rib, perhaps? The evidence of physical abuse made her heart twist.

Elizabeth continued her quick survey. Now that she had something concrete to do, some clear need to fill, the doubts were gone. Quarreling with Marx had helped, too.

"He won't be much use getting down to the river."

"No." Marx's breath was still coming in great gulps. He didn't seem to notice. He stared at his unconscious brother, eyes haunted. "We didn't make it to the pickup point in time. We were so close, dammit! So damned close!"

Elizabeth studied him. There were a dozen questions on the tip of her tongue, but only one had to be asked.

"And the other hostages?"

"The army will take care of them."

She frowned.

Marx flinched. "I set them free! I told them where to go, told them the soldiers would be looking for them. It was the best I could do."

"You set them free before you even got your brother out?"

"What did you think? That I'd just leave them there?"

The relief that washed over her erased her last, lingering doubts. She'd known he would do that, just as she'd known his threats about Niang were a ploy to ensure her help, but the relief of having that knowledge confirmed was almost overwhelming.

"That's what you wanted me to think, isn't it?" she

said accusingly. "Just like you wanted me to believe you would really harm Niang."

He went still. "I won't apologize for that. I needed your help. *Danny* needed your help. I couldn't risk you refusing." He glanced at his brother. Worry and fear shadowed his eyes. "We *still* need your help."

She rocked back on her heels, drew a deep breath. "Then we'd better get moving, hadn't we?"

While she transferred his remaining food and gear from his pack to hers, Marx cut a number of long, sturdy branches, then lashed them to the frame of his pack to form a crude litter. It wasn't pretty, but it would hold his long-limbed brother long enough to get him down that cliff. Danny gave a soft groan when they strapped him in but didn't rouse.

Elizabeth watched anxiously as Marx started the descent. The chute might be almost impossible to spot from the river, but sharp-eyed gunmen in a helicopter wouldn't miss it. They'd be shooting first and leaving questions for afterward.

She had no doubt the army would apologize profusely once they identified her body, but she didn't take much comfort from the thought.

As soon as Marx reached an outcropping of rock solid enough to hold his brother's weight, he looped the rope and signaled her to shove Danny's litter over the edge.

It was the most harrowing descent Elizabeth had ever made. With the steep, unstable slope and not enough rope, they could only move a few feet at a time. Marx had to rely on leverage and raw strength to lower the litter.

Her job was to guide it as best she could, then hold it steady while Marx moved down to the next anchorage.

Every bump wrenched a moan from the still unconscious Danny. Every moan was a reminder that there was a reason she'd waited for Marx, and it wasn't just fear.

Inch by agonizing inch, they worked their way down. Sweat streamed down her face and into her eyes, half blinding her. Her back and shoulders ached from the strain of the litter and the extra weight she carried. With each hard-fought step her world narrowed until all she could see was the few feet that divided her from Marx, all she could hear was the rasping of air in and out of her straining lungs.

She didn't hear the thump of helicopters coming their way. It was Marx's "Heads up, Bradshaw! Incoming!" that jerked her back to attention.

Desperately cursing, she tugged at the heavy litter, dragging it to the side where the rock wall and sparse shrubbery might, if she was lucky, be enough to hide it from view. Her heart was pounding so hard it felt as if it would burst out of her chest.

When the thump of the rotors drowned out even the pounding of her heart, she curled herself protectively over Danny and prayed, too frightened even to look. The muscles of her back tensed in anticipation of the bullets to come.

They never came. The sound of the helicopter faded.

Cautiously, Elizabeth removed herself from her protective crouch. The sky had never looked more gloriously empty.

"Move it!" Marx called. "We might not be so lucky the next time!"

Repressing the urge to send a shower of rubble down on him, Elizabeth moved it.

They made it to the bottom in a final scramble of curses and falling rock. Marx checked his brother, then slumped to the ground beside the litter, head down, elbows on knees, fighting for breath.

Elizabeth's fingers shook as she unbuckled her pack. Her trembling legs gave out under her first. She collapsed in an ungainly sprawl on the other side of the litter; then she wearily leaned back against the pack and stared up at the dense canopy of bamboo that arched above them, half blocking out the sky.

Why had she never noticed how really really *really* beautiful all that impenetrable green could be?

"They'll never spot us here."

Marx roused, glanced up. "No."

"You'll be sitting ducks on the river."

"While it's still light, yes. But the Pilenau army isn't properly equipped for night missions."

She stared at him, appalled. "You're not tackling that river at night!"

"I don't have a choice." He glanced at the sky again, then at his brother. He shoved to his feet. "We've got a few hours of light left. Let's not waste them arguing."

While Bradshaw tended to his brother's injuries, Derrick dug out the satellite phone. It seemed an eternity before the call went through.

"Bear."

"'Bout time you checked in." A pause. "You got your brother?"

"Yeah. A little beat up, but...he'll make it." Physically, at least. Maybe. His brother's emotional collapse would haunt him the rest of his life. He just hoped to hell it didn't haunt Danny, too. "Charley okay?"

Bear laughed. "Fine. A little disappointed at missin' you...an' not seein' more action. Didn't think much of your army friends. Said they ought to stick to knitting baby booties."

"Do they use baby booties on Pilenau?"

"Who the hell cares? He also said that unless you find someplace better, he'll meet you at the down river rendezvous point tomorrow night, 2200 sharp, like you planned."

"If I can get there."

"You'll get there," Bear assured him. Neither of them mentioned all the reasons why he might *not* be there. They didn't need to.

"You're not there," Bear added, "he'll be back the next night. That don't work..." Derrick could almost hear his friend shrug. "Well, Gerritsen said we do what we got to do."

Gerritsen was Derrick's boss and part owner of Hudson Security, whose helicopter and crew Derrick had commandeered. A strong believer in a man's responsibility to protect both his family and his business, Gerritsen would support Derrick as far as he could...and deduct the costs from his salary for the next twenty years, interest included.

"Tell him thanks," Derrick said, and meant it.

"I'll do that." Bear rang off.

Derrick tucked the phone back in his pack. There was someone to whom he owed a hell of a lot more thanks than he'd ever owe Gerritsen—she was tending to his brother right now. But two questions kept gnawing at him.

He abandoned the pack to kneel beside his brother, opposite Elizabeth. She looked up. She didn't move an inch, but he could see her withdraw before he even opened his mouth. The crusting scab on her knee glistened with fresh blood. He hated to think what her hand must be like. He didn't have the courage to look.

"Why'd you wait? Why'd you wait *here?*" Suddenly, the answers mattered intensely.

"For someone who was willing to kidnap me at gunpoint, Marx, you sure ask a lot of questions."

Her face was sweat-streaked and dirty, her hair plastered tight to her head in a ring where her hat had been. A tiny spot of blood glittered on one cheek. A cut from a twig, perhaps, or a brush with hard rock. She didn't seem to realize it was there.

Because he wanted to, and because he couldn't have stopped himself if he tried, he stretched out his hand and gently wiped away the blood with the pad of his thumb. Her skin was warm and damp beneath the dirt. Soft.

Her lips parted, ever so slightly. They'd parted just before he'd kissed her, too.

He fought against the urge to lean forward and claim another kiss. A longer kiss this time. Slower. One he could savor.

Then Danny moaned and he was jolted back to awareness of where he was. He let his hand drop.

"Sorry. Bit of blood on your cheek."

Was it his imagination, or did her lips tremble, just for an instant, before she pressed them into that implacable line? It was her eyes that gave her away. The shadows in them darkened their normal deep green to near black.

Beneath that tough exterior was a far more vulnerable woman than the one whose face she presented to the world. A woman whose life here he might well have destroyed.

Regret and guilt, however, would have to wait. He turned his attention back to his brother.

"So how is he?"

"Like you said, he'll live. But he needs to get to a doctor soon. That ankle's bad. He's got a low-grade fever that will only get worse without proper care. I've cleaned the sores and open wounds as best I could without moving him, but if we could boil some water—"

"No fire! Not here."

"No. But later, maybe." She eyed him doubtfully. "Unless you expect your friends to pluck you out of that river tonight, you'll have to make camp at some point. The nearest village with a doctor is a couple days' travel downriver. It's a good three days to the coast, maybe more." Her head tilted. He could almost see the wheels turning as she considered the options. "I assume you're not planning on going that far."

"No." Briefly, he outlined the plan. Hit the river tonight. Stop before they reached a stretch of rapids that would be too dangerous to navigate in the dark. Back on the river late afternoon tomorrow when any manhunt here would be winding down, if it wasn't already over. "By then, we should be out of range of their search. Assuming they're still looking. We have another pickup scheduled for tomorrow night. I plan to be there."

And like it or not, you'll be there with me.

He didn't say it. But he didn't plan to leave her on her own, no matter what. Earlier, he hadn't had any choice. Now, he wasn't going to give her one.

But she didn't need to know that. Not yet.

The afternoon dragged on. Elizabeth built a crude shelter over Danny to help keep off the sun. Then she settled down to watch over him. He stirred now and then but never quite roused completely. His continued unconsciousness worried her, though she didn't say anything. Marx had enough to worry about.

Once he'd sorted out the packs and equipment, Marx settled cross-legged on the ground in front of her. Just far enough away so he couldn't touch her, she noted. Far enough away that she couldn't touch him.

His face was lined, older somehow and more worn, crusted with dirt and dried sweat and the cumulative emotional and physical demands of the past two days. The past week, actually. She wondered just how much sleep he'd gotten since he first learned of his brother's capture. It couldn't have been much. He wouldn't have allowed himself the luxury of any more than the minimum necessary to keep going.

His gray eyes glittered as they met hers.

"Tell me about the river," he said. "Tell me what we'll run into tonight."

We.

The simple word made something deep within her twist with a longing so sudden and intense that she almost cried out.

Forget it. There was no *we* and never would be. She didn't say it out loud.

"I'm no expert. When I was a kid, my dad kept his camp close to the river so it would be easier to get supplies in, but these days—" She hesitated at yet another reminder of why remaining on Pilenau was so foolhardy. "These days there are too many people out there I'd just as soon not run into. I don't use the river much anymore. It's too dangerous."

Drug traffickers, timber thieves, even fleeing terrorists weren't Marx's most pressing concern, however. It was the army he needed to avoid. But traveling at night on a river in full flood simply exchanged one set of dangers for another, and she didn't know what to say that would help.

When he pressed for details on the river, she tried her best. Her best wasn't good enough. The way he shrugged, then folded up the map told her that.

"Sorry," she said.

"Don't be. You take it as it comes."

He might, Elizabeth thought grimly. He was the kind of man who would. She, on the other hand, was the kind of woman who simply ran and kept on running.

Because she couldn't help herself, she watched as he stuffed the map—*her* map—back in his pack. His hands were big with strong, callused, blunt-tipped fingers. A warrior's hands. Yet when he'd brushed her face with his thumb earlier his touch had been sure and very gentle. They were the kind of hands that could fight off the world, or gently cradle a baby while it slept.

The thought made her blink.

He sat there for a long while, his hand on the pack, his gaze distant and unfocused. She was about to ask if he was all right when he closed his eyes and slowly tilted his head forward, stretching the muscles of his back and shoulders. His soft hiss of pain said those muscles were finally rebelling against the abuse they'd taken in the last two days.

Without thinking, she rose and moved to sit behind him. Her hands were on his shoulders before she realized what she intended.

"Relax," she said when he jumped. Her voice sounded strained, even to her. Perhaps because her heart was crowding her throat.

His spine had gone straight and stiff. "I'm fine, Bradshaw. We don't—" He gasped as her fingers dug deep into the hard curve of muscle at the top of his shoulders. She eased the pressure. "You don't have—"

She dug in again, harder this time. Another gasp. His spine arched in involuntary reaction. She *did* have to. He was tired, over-strained and tense. A little massage would help.

That's what she'd tell him if he pushed it. Even if it was a lie.

She couldn't bear just watching him anymore. She *had* to touch him, if only to prove to herself she could.

Chapter 9

The cloth of his shirt was rough, damp with sweat and warm from the heat of his body. It bunched beneath her palms when she dug in, slid taut as she eased the pressure, bunched again.

The muscles beneath were like rock. Smooth, sculpted, unyielding rock.

No, not unyielding. She could feel the instant he relaxed into her touch. His small sigh of pleasure made her own breath catch.

Her fingers flexed, probed, dug for the tension deep in the muscle, close against the bone. The twinge of protest from her still-tender palm was easy to ignore.

He hadn't turned to look at her, but she knew—*knew*—that he was as intensely aware of her as she was of him.

Slowly, painstakingly, she worked her way up his shoulders to his neck, up his neck to the hard angles of his jaw and the soft, vulnerable hollows behind them.

She was having a hard time breathing.

Never before had she touched a man as she was touching Marx, not even her husband. Aaron had liked sex, but he hadn't cared for the casual intimacy of married life, the quick touch in passing, the hurried kiss as he rushed out the door to his morning classes, the slow caress that might or might not lead to sex. She'd blamed herself for Aaron's distance, but here, with Marx...

Her fingertips brushed over the pulse at Marx's throat. His heart was racing.

He jumped to his feet so quickly she almost pitched forward onto her face.

Cheeks flaming, she sank back on her heels, knotted trembling hands in her lap. She didn't dare look up. She felt a fool and a wanton and completely a woman, all at the same time. Every nerve ending in her body sang.

"Thanks. That helps. A lot. I appreciate it. Really."

Elizabeth looked up, startled. Marx was *babbling*. For the first time since she'd dropped out of that tree with her rifle pointed at his heart, he was rattled. By *her*.

Her hands stopped trembling. In spite of herself, she smiled.

Marx stalked away, only to be brought up short by the cliff. He glared as if it had deliberately gotten in his way. Then he spun on his heel and stomped off toward the river, muttering under his breath.

When all she could hear was the soft rustling of the bamboo and the thudding of her own heart, Elizabeth forced herself to move at last. There was still work to be done, after all, and an injured man to care for. She needed to remember that.

By the time Marx finally reappeared, she'd had

plenty of time to regret her rashness and to imagine, in exquisite detail, what it would have been like to touch him without the barrier of his shirt between them.

The wayward direction her thoughts had taken made her prickly and defensive. She needn't have worried. One look at Marx's face told her he'd withdrawn into himself. *He* would keep a safe emotional distance between them even if she couldn't.

"How's Danny?"

"Better. He roused a bit a few minutes ago."

"What'd he say?" The mingled hope and fear in his voice made her ache.

"That he was thirsty," she said gently, knowing what he was really asking. "He asked for you."

He didn't need to know that his brother had been only partially conscious when he'd called for him, or that Danny had sounded lost and frightened and very, very young. Once he'd taken the small sip of water Elizabeth had allowed him, he'd looked around him vaguely, clearly seeking his brother. When Marx hadn't been there, he'd whispered, "Please tell him I'm sorry." He hadn't had the strength for more.

She couldn't tell Marx that, either.

"I told him you'd be right back," she said. "Then I gave him a drink of water, a little one, and that was it. He's asleep, now."

Marx sank to the ground beside his brother. "I should have been here."

"He's a grown man, Marx, no matter what you think. Don't waste time blaming yourself for the mistakes he made…or yourself for the mistakes *you* made, either."

"What would *you* know about it?"

Everything. "Don't snarl at me!"

"I'm not snarling!"

"The hell you're not!"

"I— Ah, hell!" Anger drove him back to his feet. For an instant, she thought he was going to stalk away again.

She was wrong. Marx wasn't the kind of man who allowed his emotions to rule for long. With a clear effort, he got a rein on his anger.

"We should rest while we still can," he said, every word carefully controlled. "You sack out for a while. I'll keep watch."

Elizabeth shook her head. "I can't sleep in the afternoon." It wasn't quite a lie. Right now, she was too tired to deal with the dreams that sleep usually brought. Last night's dreamless sleep was an aberration and unlikely to be repeated.

The memory of waking with Marx's body curled warm and strong against hers was still achingly vivid…and best forgotten.

Still, he hesitated. Derrick Marx, bearer of the world's sins, couldn't allow himself to rest if others hadn't first.

"You promise you'll wake me if—"

"The world won't stop turning just because you're not watching it for an hour or two." Easier to be sarcastic than kind and much, much safer.

He stood, clearly reluctant, then glanced back down at her. "You're sure—"

"Go to sleep, Marx. Don't let the bedbugs bite."

His only response was an irritated grunt. Elizabeth watched him walk away.

She had been in her twenties when she'd first heard that childhood warning about bedbugs that bit. By the time she was three, though, she could identify all the creepy crawly things in the jungle that she really *did* have to worry about. Her father had made sure of that.

Out of the depths of his inconsolable grief at the death of his wife, the mother she scarcely remembered, her father had turned all his energies to his research and to teaching her about the orchids that had become more important to him than anything else in the world, including his own daughter.

It wasn't his fault he hadn't had any talent for nursery rhymes. Or being a father. Or leaving.

Amazing how much like him she'd become, especially considering how badly she'd once wanted to get away.

The sharp stab of pain as she unconsciously dug her nails into her battered palm made her jump. She dragged in air, slowly forced her hands to unclench and her back to straighten.

Marx chose a spot in the shade where fallen bamboo leaves had drifted into a heap. There wasn't quite enough space for his long body, but he curled up on his side, head pillowed on one arm, his rifle cradled against him like a lover. After one last glance around to assure himself that all was well, he closed his eyes and was almost instantly asleep.

Because there was nothing else to do, Elizabeth sat

right where she was, watching him sleep, trying desperately not to think of anything at all.

Derrick awoke to the sound of laughter.

He kept his eyes shut, wondering if he was just dreaming he was awake. His senses told him he was right where he expected to be, but…laughter?

Then it came again. This time he was awake enough to hear the strain in it, the rough edges caused by pain.

He opened his eyes to see Bradshaw, cross-legged on the ground beside his brother, a gentle, almost wistful smile softening her face. Her left hand was laced in Danny's, her head bent as though she'd leaned closer to catch his words.

Danny was awake and smiling and talking. Too low for Derrick to catch the words.

Relief surged through him. But the relief was followed by a wave of irritation. His brother was awake and, despite everything he'd gone through, flirting with the first pretty girl he saw. Flirting with *Bradshaw*.

He should have remembered that Danny had all the charm in the family. It was part of what had gotten him into trouble in the first place.

Derrick shoved his rifle aside—even in his sleep he'd kept his hand curled over the stock—and got to his feet.

"About time you woke up, little brother," he said dryly.

The smile on Danny's face went crooked, trembled. "I was thinking…the same about you, big brother."

He tugged his hand free from Bradshaw's, started to hold it out, then quickly withdrew it.

Derrick was down on his knees in an instant. He grabbed Danny's hand and held on tight.

"You must be doing okay if you're already putting the moves on Bradshaw," he said roughly. Derrick smiled, felt the corners of the smile waver. It was the sunlight that made his eyes water. Only the sunlight.

"You know me." Danny didn't even try to smile.

"Yeah. You always were the tough one in the family."

He released his brother's hand, rocked back on his heels.

"Up for a bit of rafting?"

"Elizabeth— Dr. Bradshaw. She was just…telling me. About the raft." Danny grimaced. "Guess I should have gone to that kids' boot camp thing, after all. Like you wanted me to."

Guilt stabbed deeper, twisting in Derrick's gut. "And I should have paid more attention to what *you* wanted, little brother. I'm sorry I didn't."

"No, I—"

Bradshaw jumped to her feet, shattering the moment.

"We need to eat," she said briskly. "All of us."

"Right." Embarrassed, Derrick gave his brother a crooked smile. "I'll let you kick me later, okay?"

There'd be time to make right all the things he'd done wrong. Pray, God. Years and years and years. There was a lot he had to make up for.

Danny's smile wavered. "Sure." He couldn't quite meet Derrick's gaze when he said it.

Marx was inflating the raft when Elizabeth emerged from the bamboo onto the rocky edge of the Ipona. He'd hacked down some bamboo, then propped it up like walls around the raft to make it look as if the thicket extended farther than it did. As camouflage, it wasn't great, but she supposed it would serve. If no one came too close or looked too hard.

Marx didn't even glance up when she plopped down on the rocks nearby. She laid her rifle on the ground beside her.

How long had it been since she'd last done anything without having her rifle close at hand? she wondered, then decided she didn't really want to know.

The steady huff of the hand pump seemed unnaturally loud.

"Danny asleep again?" Marx didn't miss a beat.

"Yes. His fever's a little higher. Not bad, but…" She let the rest trail away unsaid.

"He'll be fine. He's tough. Always has been."

Elizabeth didn't bother responding. She wasn't the one Marx was trying to convince.

He pushed harder on the pump. Up. Down. Up. Down. Trying to lose himself in the mindlessness of repetitive physical labor.

"You're crazy to try that river at night," she said.

He prodded the sides of the raft, resumed the relentless pumping. "Probably. But tomorrow night, unless I can find a better spot before then, Charley's going to be downriver to pick us up. I intend to be there waiting when he does. And you and Danny are going to be there, too, waiting right beside me."

"I'm not crazy like you, Marx."

He didn't look up. His jaw was set so hard it made rock look soft. "No, you're crazier. And I'm not giving you a choice, Bradshaw."

"I told you. I'm not going with you."

"Why not?"

Because I can't! Because I no longer have the courage to try! "Pilenau's my home. I grew up here."

"And left. Once."

Elizabeth flinched. "Exactly." Then, as the implications of his words sank in, "How did you know I'd left?"

"*Doctor* Bradshaw? You didn't get that in Pilenau. Besides, I looked you up on the Internet."

"Me?"

"If you weren't buried here in this damned jungle, you'd know it's not so easy to hide anymore. Not even here on Pilenau."

"I'm not hiding!"

He shrugged.

Curiosity got the best of her. Curiosity…and fear. Just what *did* he know about her? "So what did it say? About me, I mean."

"Not much, really. Date of birth. Degrees. List of publications." He scowled. "I couldn't even pronounce half the titles."

"That's it?"

"Pretty much. You were mentioned in a few newspaper articles about jungle rescues and credited with helping a dozen or so scientific expeditions."

He stopped pumping, his attention all on her now. The intensity of his gaze made her breath catch.

She shouldn't have brought it up. She started to get to her feet.

"It didn't tell me any of the important things about you," he said softly.

She sank back. The pit of her stomach had suddenly fallen away. "Like…what?"

He set the pump aside, leaned toward her. "It didn't tell me that you're prickly and brave and as hardheaded and independent as they come."

His voice was low, a little rough, yet soft as a caress. She shivered. He was so close she could have sworn he'd touched her, and her skin was heating in response.

"It didn't tell me that you're kind. That you'll risk your life to help another, even if he doesn't deserve it."

He leaned closer still, stretched out a hand, and gently brushed back one of those impossible locks of hair that were always getting free of her ponytail.

"The smart part I could guess," he said. His hand cupped the side of her face. "But it didn't tell me that you're beautiful."

Elizabeth licked lips suddenly gone dry, fought for air.

The edge of his thumb traced the line of her lips, brushed at the moisture she'd just left there. His eyes held her pinned in place like a moth.

"It didn't tell me why you're so afraid to leave," he said.

With a choked cry of protest, Elizabeth rocketed to her feet. He was up even faster, blocking her escape.

"Bradshaw… *Elizabeth*. Listen to me," he pleaded.

She spun, intending to run away. The unmistakable

whump-whump-whump of a helicopter coming over the ridge behind them stopped her dead in her tracks.

"Shit!" Marx lunged for her, dragging her down, deeper into the bamboo. Rocks and the hacked-off stumps of the bamboo he'd chopped down gouged her back and side. She flung out her hand to brace herself and gasped as her injured palm scraped over hard rock. She felt the sudden wet heat of blood.

Later.

"My rifle!" she cried. It lay on the rocks not inches from where she'd been sitting. It might have been on the other side of the moon.

"Forget your rifle!" Marx had his in his hands. He craned to get a better view. "Shit! Bastard's coming this way!"

The *whump-whump-whump* grew louder.

Elizabeth turned, looking for a means to escape. No way through the bamboo. Run along it and she'd either be in the river or on exposed rock.

Marx's hand closed over her shoulder. "Don't move. That bamboo I staked out over the raft won't fool him long, but he's looking for movement, for people running away, not for what might be a fisherman's shelter or something."

"Or something," Elizabeth spat. Her heart felt as if it were battering its way out of her chest. She was sweating, and not from the heat. Without her rifle, she felt naked. "I should have shot you the minute you walked into my camp."

He glanced back at her. She'd swear he almost smiled. "Next time, you'll know."

Whump-whump-whump-whump-whump. The thing was almost on top of them, moving low and slow. Whoever was in the chopper would spot the raft for sure.

All she could see was Marx's broad back and shoulders, his face in profile, hard with determination.

"There's going to be a next time?"

"Nah," he said lightly. "I'm not planning on coming back to Pilenau. You'll have to shoot the next guy, instead."

"Pity," she said, fighting to keep her voice just as light as he'd kept his.

Fear had wrapped around her insides so tightly she was finding it hard to breathe. She wanted to lean against him, wanted to feel his solid strength so she'd know it was going to be all right. She wanted to curl into a ball right here and let whatever was going to happen, happen. She wanted to grab her rifle and run out on those rocks and dare whoever was in that chopper to shoot her.

Maybe she'd finally gone crazy, after all, just as she'd always feared.

He hadn't removed his hand from her shoulder. It was like an anchor, keeping her steady. She breathed deeply, reaching for calm. Listening.

The chopper wasn't coming any closer. It wasn't moving away, either.

"Marx? What's happening? What are they doing?"

"Waiting for someone to move."

"What about Danny?"

His fingers dug into her shoulder. "Pray he doesn't move, either."

A burst of gunfire shattered the still air. For an instant, Elizabeth thought she saw rocks dancing across the river bank; then Marx threw himself on top of her and she couldn't see anything except bamboo stubble and her newly injured hand just inches from her face. The blood, she noted distantly, was already drawing flies.

"Don't. Move."

Elizabeth squirmed, trying to get free of his weight. "They've already seen us!"

"No, they haven't. That was just a little exploratory shooting. They want to see if they can flush anyone out of the bushes. You move and they'll *really* start shooting."

Another sweeping burst of automatic fire. This time the bullets stitched through Marx's makeshift bamboo screen from right to left, *tat-tat-tat-tat-tat*. Chips of rock went zinging, almost as deadly as the bullets themselves. Marx curled his body tighter around hers, shielding her from the flying rock. She could feel his breath warm on the side of her face, the rapid rise and fall of his chest against her back.

There was a sudden whoosh of air under pressure, abruptly released. At least one of the bullets had hit the raft, maybe more.

"Shit!"

Another burst of gunfire, another whoosh.

"Shit shit shit shit *shit!*"

The gunner let off one last round before the chopper rose, moving away. Marx kept her pinned and motionless for another minute or two. Then he rolled aside and let her up.

"You okay?"

"Fine. I'm…fine."

She couldn't stop the quaver in her voice. Her gaze was fixed on the raft not five feet from them. A few minutes ago it had been almost filled, its sides round and taut from the air inside. Now one side was completely flat, the bullet holes in the tough fabric gaping and black.

Marx stared at it grimly. "Guess we should be grateful they were too lazy to land that chopper. Still…" He shook his head and got to his feet. "I'm going to check on Danny."

"Sure." She couldn't take her eyes off that flattened raft. So close. The bullets had come so *close*.

She shakily climbed to her feet, then retrieved her rifle. A chip of flying rock had scraped the stock, but otherwise it was undamaged. The familiar weight and feel of it was almost comforting.

For an instant, she debated following Marx but decided he'd call her if he needed her. In the meantime, there was a raft that needed repairing.

Marx, thank God, had come prepared. She'd already cut and glued the first patch when he came back, his arm around his brother. Danny's face was white and drawn with strain, but with his brother's help he was managing to limp along on the crude leg brace better than she'd have expected.

He shook off Marx's arm and eased down onto the ground. Sweat beaded his brow from the effort of moving. He was breathing hard, but he managed a wobbly grin.

"You okay?" she asked.

"Fine. Sort of." He spotted her rifle on the ground just inches from her hand. The grin faded. "For a minute there, I was almost homesick for that cage I'd been living in. I thought they were shooting at me."

"They were," said Marx.

Danny looked up. It was clear it cost him an effort to meet his brother's gaze, but this time he didn't look away. "I know."

Four words, Elizabeth thought. Two each. And a thousand that still waited to be said. But as with so much else, now was not the time, and this was not the place.

Marx squatted beside her. His eyes were shadowed with worry, yet somehow, with him so close, her own worries faded.

"How about you?" he said softly. "How are you doing?"

"Fine. Thanks." She managed a slight smile. "Your raft's not doing so well, however."

His own smile banished the shadows and made her heart lift.

"Yeah. Damned unfriendly of them to wait until I'd almost finished filling it." He didn't even glance at the raft.

Her lungs constricted. Again.

Desperate for distraction, she snatched up one of the patches she'd been working on, held it up. "Have a patch. I already trimmed it to fit."

He didn't glance at the patch, either. He was looking

at her, nothing but her. His gaze slid over her face, as intimate and gentle as a caress, then fixed on her mouth.

Elizabeth licked lips suddenly gone dry.

"Marx?"

Those gray eyes lifted, locked with hers. "It's going to be all right," he said softly. "Trust me."

"I do," she said. It was barely a whisper. She cleared her throat. "I do trust you, Marx. Damned if I know why."

Again that smile that shot right through her. "Damned if I know, either," he said.

Then he stretched out his hand and gently brushed back a damp lock of hair plastered along her cheek.

"I'm also damned if I know why you bother with that ugly ponytail. Drives me crazy, the way your hair keeps slipping out like that."

She gave a shaky laugh. "My orchids don't mind."

He snorted. "Orchids! You deserve a hell of a lot better than orchids! You—"

A small grunt of pain from behind them cut off whatever he was going to say. Startled, Elizabeth whirled to find Danny staring at them. She'd forgotten he even existed.

"Sorry," he said, red-faced. "I was looking for a softer rock to sit on."

Marx's mouth twisted in a rueful grimace. "You find one, you let me know. In the meantime…" He turned back to the damaged raft. He deliberately didn't look at her. "Bradshaw? You still have that patch?"

"Uh…sure." She'd let it fall on the rocks at her feet and never noticed.

Annoyed—at herself, at him, at how easily he could distract her—she handed him the patch, then went to tend to his brother. The sooner the man was out of her life, the better.

Despite Danny's protests that he was fine, really, she forced him to swallow more pills for the pain. The adrenaline rush that had carried him through the attack was already wearing off, leaving him paler and shakier than before. She didn't want to think of the condition he'd be in after a night on the river.

"Thanks," he said as she helped him settle into a more comfortable position propped against his brother's pack. "For everything."

She forced an encouraging smile. "It's going to be okay, you know." *Please please* please *let that be the truth. For all of us.*

"I know. I really messed up but Der—" He glanced at his brother's broad back. "Der'll sort it out. He always does somehow. If only I'd listened, maybe—"

"*If only* are two words you should learn to avoid. Trust me on that one." She gave his shoulder a reassuring squeeze. "Try to rest if you can. You've got a long night ahead of you."

Marx didn't even look up when she rejoined him. She settled as far from him as she could. It wasn't far enough.

She wanted to talk, if for no other reason than to hear the sound of his voice. Talking would be so much easier than thinking about what had almost happened, what could still happen.

She had so many questions. She wanted to ask Marx

why he'd never married. She wanted to ask about the little things, like what kind of music he listened to, what kinds of books he read, what he did in his spare time.

She wanted to just sit there and watch him, storing up the intimate details that made memory come alive.

She refused to think about anyone's leaving, his… or hers.

"There's at least six holes on your end, Bradshaw," Marx growled. "You want to get them done before next week, you'd better start patching."

Chapter 10

The patches were holding. For now, anyway.

Derrick frowned at the raft without really seeing it. They'd waited until the sun had disappeared over the treetops before moving the raft out from under its flimsy bamboo cover. Bradshaw had helped him pull it down to the river's edge before going back to check on Danny, while Derrick loaded the gear and strapped it down.

According to her, Danny was awake and his fever was down. Whatever combination of pills and native potions she'd poured down him seemed to be helping. A little food and being free of that bamboo prison had probably helped a bit, too. Hope was a powerful restorative.

None of which meant Danny was ready to tackle what lay ahead. Bradshaw *had* to come with them, for Danny's sake if not for her own. He couldn't handle the raft and Danny, too.

Derrick dragged out the satellite phone, but Bear had no help to offer.

"Sorry, man. Charley's rarin' to go, but—" The satellite lag made the pause stretch agonizingly. "The army guys in Pilenau City are plenty grateful for the help. They got all the hostages just fine. They're not complainin' about having a few less terrorists to deal with, either. But the guys on the ground— Der, I gotta tell you. Their blood's up. They want everyone, and I mean *everyone,* you and Danny included."

Derrick swore. "They got our names?"

"Not so far. But now that they've got the hostages safe, they're not interested in names, Der. They're interested in body counts."

"Shit."

"How's Danny?"

"Better." Derrick hesitated. "But another twenty-four of being slammed around won't do him any good."

Another pause that wasn't a result of lag time alone. Then, "Kid's tougher than you give him credit for."

"Yeah."

The silence stretched.

"You find a place where Charley can put down," Bear said at last, "Charley'll find you."

"I'm counting on it."

More than he cared to admit, Derrick thought as he stuck the phone back in its pocket. Just as he'd been counting on Bradshaw more than he should have.

"Any news?"

Derrick jumped. He hadn't heard her come up behind him.

He turned to face her and bit back an oath. She already had her pack on her back. If she were going with them, she would have loaded it on the raft with his.

"The army got the hostages out safely. *All* of them."

"That's good." She frowned. "What about your friend with the helicopter?"

"He'll be waiting for us as planned unless we can find a safe pickup point sooner." He glanced at the lengthening shadows, then at the cliff at their backs. "Might as well get going."

"Yes." She seemed more subdued than relieved, Derrick thought. Tired, probably. Ready to have him out of her life. "You're crazy to stay here, you know."

She nodded. "Yes. And you're crazy to tackle that river."

"At least we agree on some things." He paused a beat. "Want a ride across the river?"

"In *that* thing? You'll be a mile downstream before you can get to the other side, and where would that leave me?"

"A mile downstream…with dry feet?"

She laughed and her whole face lit up.

"You ought to laugh more often."

He watched as the light faded from her face.

"There are a lot of things I ought to do more often," she said sadly.

For a moment, she simply stood there, staring at him. As if she were trying to memorize him, Derrick thought, puzzled. He'd rather have just kissed her. That kiss he'd claimed when they'd parted had been too quick. He wanted more. More time. More heat. More…*her.*

He wanted, beyond everything else, to keep her safe. That he was the one who had put her at such risk was just one of those vicious jokes that life played on you when you least expected it.

"You get your brother," she said. "I'll put your raft in the water."

He knew when argument was useless.

Danny was awake and waiting. He didn't look any better. On the other hand, he didn't look any worse, either.

"Ready?" Derrick asked.

"Ready." Danny gave him a weak smile. "But you're going to have to help me up."

By the time they had reached the river's edge, Danny was shaking from the effort and breathing hard. He eyed the raft that now danced on the river's muddy waters, impatiently tugging at the rope that Bradshaw, with feet braced against the current, held tight with both hands.

"A bath *and* a ride," he said. "What more could a guy ask for?"

"A cold beer?"

Danny's laugh ended on a gasp of pain. "Make it a six-pack and you're on."

"Two. With all the barbecued ribs you can eat." Why had he never realized just how gutsy his little brother was?

They were both half-soaked by the time Danny had stretched out awkwardly on the bottom of the raft. Derrick clambered in after, taking his place at the stern seat. He turned to Bradshaw, who was struggling against the stronger pull of the now heavier raft, and extended his hand.

"I owe you!"

"Damn right you do!" She ignored his hand, ready to toss the rope into the raft and set them free.

He grabbed her wrist on the swing and yanked.

Bradshaw tottered. The river snatched her feet from under her. Derrick gave one great heave and hauled her on board. She tumbled into a sprawling heap beside Danny, kicking and swearing.

"Marx, you bastard!"

"Not now, Bradshaw!" He snatched up the paddle and straightened the spinning raft, pointing its nose downriver, into the heart of the current.

The river greedily snatched them up. In the deepening dusk, it seemed a vast, gray plain, quieter here in the center than it had seemed when they waited on its banks. Quieter and far more overwhelming.

They had maybe ten more minutes of this dull gray light, then nothing but stars to show them the way. Moonrise was a half hour away, and even that wouldn't do them much good if the clouds moved in to blot it out.

"Keep an eye out for snags!" he shouted, digging in the paddle to keep the raft pointed straight ahead. One half-submerged rock or tree root could rip the bottom out of it.

"We can't see snags in the dark!" Bradshaw shouted back.

"Then pray!"

She shot him a venomous look but didn't waste time arguing. The venom, he thought, was only partial cover for the very real fear he sensed in her. She *was* afraid to leave. He was sure of it. What he didn't know was why.

Taking care not to unbalance them, she slithered out of her pack, lashed it beside his and settled herself on the seat with her back to him to keep watch. Even in the gathering gloom he could see the tension in her hunched shoulders.

From his sprawled position in the bottom of the raft, Danny watched the exchange and tried to keep out of their way. Derrick gave him a reassuring grin. He wasn't sure it carried much conviction.

As always in the jungle, there was no slow transition from dusk to dark. One minute he could see, if only vaguely. The next, everything had gone black except for the glittering stars.

Derrick tilted his head back, studying the diamond-studded vault of sky above them and the scattered blobs of black where clouds blocked the light. Not as many clouds as the night before. With any luck, it wouldn't rain.

As his eyes adjusted, he could make out the occasional black against black on the river that meant they weren't the only things adrift on the Ipona. Every now and then he caught the faint, glinting reflection of starlight on the water. He could dimly make out the darker black of the trees on the river's banks that were now the boundaries of their world. They seemed farther away than they really were.

And there, straight ahead in the center of his suddenly narrow little world, he could see the huddled shadow that was Bradshaw, keeping watch.

Had he done the right thing by snatching her away? Had he had a choice?

He wanted to touch her. He wanted to reassure her, promise her he'd take care of her and keep her safe.

He wanted to kiss her, as he'd kissed her there at the top of the cliff.

He wanted to make love to her, somewhere private and safe.

"Shadow ahead on your right, maybe twenty yards," she called. They were the first words she'd spoken for some time. In the dark, her voice sounded hushed and distant. "Tree, I think. It's big."

With a silent curse, he dug the paddle into the river and steered them away. They passed it a couple of minutes later. It was a tree—a big one—and a hell of a lot closer than he'd have liked. Caught on submerged rocks, probably, waiting for the tug of the current to break it free. Hopefully, it would stay stuck until they were far enough downriver that it couldn't run them down.

The moon was just cresting the treetops when he caught the distant sound of a helicopter.

"Marx!" "Der!" The chorused warning sounded suddenly, unnaturally loud.

"I hear it! We'll head for the trees, get under their cover." He started paddling hard, driving the raft across the current toward the closest shelter available.

In the bottom of the raft, Danny stirred, straining to see behind them.

"Probably headed back to Pilenau City!" Derrick called, and tried to sound as if he believed it.

Danny sat up straighter. "Then why are they using a searchlight to scan the river?"

Derrick glanced back over his shoulder. Maybe a quarter mile behind them he could see the harsh white beam of a high-powered searchlight playing across the surface of the water.

He cursed and paddled faster.

They made the shelter of the overhanging trees just in time.

"Grab any overhanging branches you can find, see if you can hold us!" Derrick shouted. "River's still running fast so the bank's probably too steep for us to beach!"

He couldn't see a damn thing in the black on black under the trees, but branches whipped his face as the river pulled them past. He grabbed, felt leaves peel off in his hands, grabbed again, then again.

"Got it!" Bradshaw crowed. "Shit! Hold it! Hold your end!" she added as the current threatened to swing them around.

Derrick grabbed, and this time he caught a branch that was big enough and strong enough to hold against their weight.

"Heads down!" he called as the searchlight swung toward them.

He hunched his shoulders and prayed the branch wouldn't break under the strain. If they drifted back out into the open river, they'd be sitting ducks.

The sound of the engines got louder and louder, but all his attention was focused on that stark beam of light sweeping across the water, left, right, left, coming closer with every pass. It hit their hiding place a moment later, a little in front of them but not by much. The low-hanging branches sheltering them suddenly arced black against white. Blobs of light swum in a dizzying pattern across the churning surface of the water.

Derrick had a brief glimpse of the crumbling, muddy

wall of the bank above them and the dangerous tangle of drifting branches caught against it, then the searchlight swung away, leaving him blinded by the afterimage burned on his retinas.

When he could see again, he shifted his grip on the branch, then craned to peer out at the receding light. "We'll give 'em another few minutes, then we'll go."

"They know we're here." Danny's voice was scarcely a whisper, but Derrick caught every word, even above the hammering of his own heart.

"No, they don't. They're fishing, just in case. I'd do the same."

But he'd been hoping the Pilenau army would follow their usual pattern of going for the fast and easy and ignoring the less likely possibilities. Just his bad luck the team sent to close down the Sword's camp had someone in charge who believed in covering all the bases…and didn't listen to headquarters.

Once back on the river, he kept closer to shore, but the helicopter didn't return. None of them spoke. After the terror of that brief encounter, there was nothing to say that they wanted to put into words.

The moon was still riding high in the sky when Derrick decided it was time to quit. He didn't dare risk the rapids that lay ahead. Besides, he was bone tired, and tired men made mistakes.

He glanced at his brother. Danny hadn't said a word since they'd taken refuge under the trees. Derrick rolled his aching shoulders wearily. He wasn't the only one who needed rest.

"Bradshaw?"

She didn't glance back. "What?"

"Keep your eyes peeled for some place we can put ashore."

"What am I supposed to look for? Neon signs? Flashing arrows saying, 'Hotel and restaurant this way?'" Beneath the sarcasm, Derrick could hear the weary strain in her voice.

"Sure. A steak house would be nice, too."

All the answer he got was a not-so-ladylike snort of disgust.

Cautiously, he guided the raft in closer. Even in the moonlight, the shoreline was a faceless, formless black wall, as unwelcoming as it was impenetrable. Each time he'd spotted anything that looked as though it might serve, the current had already swept them past.

In the end, he had no choice but to bring them up close enough so that the blackness resolved itself into the looming curves of trees and underbrush and the harder mass of unforgiving rock. He'd almost decided that they'd have to tie up under the trees and simply sleep in the raft when Bradshaw suddenly leaned forward, eagerly pointing.

"There! See? That narrow strip of gray. It might be a gravel bench where animals come down to drink."

He saw it, swung closer to shore and almost missed it.

"Grab those branches!"

Bradshaw was braced and ready. Even Danny, roused by the shouts, dragged himself onto his knees so he could grab for whatever came within reach.

The raft lurched, then spun as it struck something in the water. If they went too far, they'd never get back.

"Hold on! Now! Now!"

Derrick drove the raft into the shore, fighting against the current. He saw Danny grab for a handhold, heard his grunt of pain at the effort. Bradshaw was half standing on the seat, desperately trying to wrap her arms around a branch strong enough to hold them. Derrick tossed the paddle aside and grabbed for a branch of his own.

The raft came to a halt with a jerk, but the tug on Derrick's arms said the current was strong here.

"Danny! Dig out the flashlight in the top pocket of my pack. Bradshaw! Grab the bow rope. As soon as Danny can show us what we've got, tie us up to the first big tree you can reach."

They'd been lucky. By the light of the flashlight he saw they'd managed to stop beneath a steep, muddy bank choked with ferns, scrubby bushes and the exposed roots of an old tree that was gradually being undermined by the river. Eventually, the river would eat away enough of the bank to take the tree with it, but for now, the old giant would hold and the roots would provide them a way up the bank.

The current tugged at the raft, trying to snatch them away again. He couldn't hold it for long. The river was clearly deep here and the current wouldn't willingly let them go. He looped the stern rope around the branch above him and knotted it quickly.

"Bradshaw?" She was staring at the crumbling mud bank as if she'd seen a ghost. "Ready?" he asked.

She started guiltily, then nodded.

"Get up that bank as quick as you can and tie us off. As soon as you're done, I'll follow with the stern rope, then work my way back along the bank as far as I can. When I can't go any farther, I'll tie up the stern and give a shout so you can release the bow. We may have to do a little hopscotching, but that way we should be able to tow Danny and the raft back to that gravel bar without risk of losing them. Easier that than trying to paddle against the current. We'll set up camp on the bar, and pray the river doesn't rise any higher. Understand?"

She nodded again, distantly, as if she weren't really listening.

"What about me?" Danny demanded.

"We're going to swap places. Once Bradshaw's up that bank, I'll take her place and pass her the bow rope. Whatever you do, don't drop the flashlight! We haven't gone too far, but with this kind of undergrowth we can't move an inch without light."

He checked the knot on the rope he'd fastened around the branch, then carefully edged to the side of the raft so Danny could lever himself onto the seat. The raft bobbed and bucked beneath them, fighting the current and the ropes restraining it.

"Okay, Bradshaw. I'll hold the raft as steady as I can. Ready?"

She didn't look at him. "There's an orchid on that bank," she said. It came out as little more than a whisper. "See? There, beside that fern. The spray of small white flowers?"

Derrick bent to her, startled. "Bradshaw?"

No response.

He touched her shoulder. It was like touching a wire drawn tight to the point of snapping.

Really worried now, he gave her a little shake. "Bradshaw?"

She shuddered, then drew in her breath and straightened, blinking madly.

He leaned closer without letting her go. "You okay?"

She glanced at him, looked away. "Yeah. Sure," she mumbled. "Fine."

"You don't have to—"

"Don't drop the rope." Then she grabbed hold of one of the exposed roots and swung off the raft, setting it to bobbing drunkenly.

She tested each foot and handhold, but twice the root she'd chosen broke under her. With each shift in weight, each lunge upward, some of the rain-soaked soil beneath those anchoring roots gave way, falling into the roiling water in a splattering shower of mud, broken roots and debris that was instantly swept away.

Just before the top, she hesitated, her attention clearly caught by the lone orchid that gleamed stark white amid the shadowy black humps of root and rock. Derrick was about to call up to her when she dragged her gaze from the orchid to scramble up the last few feet and over the top.

"Toss up the rope." She was on her stomach, half hanging over the edge of the bank. In the harsh brightness of the flashlight, her eyes were black hollows in a face bleached of color and life.

Just a trick of the light, Derrick told himself. *She's tired. We're all tired.*

The first toss fell short. With Danny's help, Derrick pulled the rope back in the raft, looped it and tried again. The second time it snagged on one of the overhanging branches. He tried a third time.

"Got it!"

Bradshaw coiled the rope up and cautiously started to her feet. With a weary sigh, half the riverbank gave way beneath her.

Chapter 11

Elizabeth hit the water in an avalanche of mud and rocks and uprooted scrub. The current hungrily snatched her up and tumbled her away. She couldn't breathe, couldn't think, couldn't even tell up from down. Her eyes were wide open, yet she was blind. Her ears were filled with a gurgling rush that blotted out every sound.

Was this what it had been like for Shanna?

How long did it take to drown?

Her tumbling stopped with a jerk that almost pulled her arm out of its socket.

The rope! She hadn't let go!

Her grip tightened convulsively. Something slammed into her, scratching and clawing at her face and arm.

Frantically, she tried to twist free. The thing grabbed her shoulder, raked down her back. With her free hand she fumbled, wrenched it off. It had already spun away when her sluggish brain finally identified it as a chunk of brushwood that had fallen into the river with her.

The rope jerked again, insistently pulling her back, into the current.

Marx!

Another twisted root slammed into her, gouging her side, scraping down her leg.

It would be so easy to let go.

Her lungs squeezed, demanding air. She clamped her jaws shut against the urge and kicked in the direction she hoped was up.

I'd never be able to face him again if I just gave up and drowned.

Some distant part of her brain said there was a flaw in that argument somewhere, but she didn't care. She wasn't giving up. Marx wouldn't let her. Shanna wouldn't want her to. *She* didn't want to. She knew that now, when it was almost too late.

Blind, deaf, disoriented, yet suddenly determined, she flailed against the tumbling current, fighting to grab the rope with both hands, fighting to hold on because *he* was on the other end.

She could *feel* the forward movement now, the water parting around her like waves before the bow of a boat. And then a hand clamped on the back of her shirt and dragged her up and she was sprawling over the side of the raft, retching water and gasping for air.

She was still choking and coughing up water when Marx dragged her all the way into the raft.

"Dammit, Bradshaw!" His hands closed over her shoulders, pulling her upright. He gave her an angry shake. "What the hell did you think you were doing?"

She tried to brush back the dripping wet hair plastered across her face. "I didn't—"

He gave her another, harder shake. "You scared the hell out of me!"

And then he wrapped his arms around her and dragged her to him, holding her tight. Holding her safe.

With a whimper of relief, she sagged against him and burst into tears.

His hand trembled as he pressed her head down against his chest. "It's okay," he murmured, and brushed a kiss against her forehead. "It's okay. You're safe."

The tears eventually receded, leaving her drained. Her eyelids burned, her throat hurt, but Marx still held her close. Slowly, he stroked the palm of his hand up and down her arm.

Reluctantly, she pushed away. Without the protective heat of his body, the night air seemed suddenly chill on her wet skin. She shivered.

"Thanks." She couldn't quite meet his gaze. Despite the cold, her bare skin still glowed where his palm had stroked it.

She dragged in a lungful of air and slowly let it out. Amazing how...*miraculous*...such a simple thing as breathing could seem. Some miracles, however, would have to wait.

"Help me up, will you?" she said and was pleased the words came out so steadily. She carefully didn't glance at Marx. "After all this, I think I spotted a better way up that bank."

It took maybe half an hour to work their way back along the overgrown riverbank. It wasn't the distance that slowed them down, but all the treacherous rocks and roots and bushes that lurked in the darkness, just waiting to trip them and send them plunging back into the river.

Elizabeth was intensely grateful for all of it because it kept her from thinking. One foot, then the next. One handhold after another, inch by inch by inch. She was almost sorry when she stepped out of the trees and onto the thread of ground they'd been aiming for.

The gravelly sand beach was long but so narrow and overshadowed with trees it wouldn't be easily visible from above, even if the river were lower. If there'd been more rain upriver, it would probably be underwater by now.

As it was, the trees were so close and thick that they seemed to blot out half the sky. It was sheer luck she'd spotted the place. Even if the army were still looking for them, which she doubted, no one in a helicopter cruising above the treetops, searchlight avidly cutting the dark, would even suspect this place existed.

While Marx helped his brother up to higher ground, then rigged a tarp shelter for him, Elizabeth wearily dragged the raft up under the trees out of the river's reach and tied it up. Her head pounded and every inch of her body protested the abuse of the past two days. She longed for dry clothes but lacked the energy to bother. Easier just to shed her wet ones once she'd made her bed and sleep in the nude. Dry clothes could wait till morning.

Still, she was as grateful for the work and the discomfort as she'd been for that fight to get back along the riverbank—they kept her from thinking too much, remembering too much.

They didn't, however, keep her from an intense, skin-pricking awareness of Derrick Marx as she helped settle an exhausted Danny under the shelter. A small flashlight, carefully hooded, provided only meager light. Meager, but more than enough to highlight the shadows in Marx's face, the stubble of beard along his jaw, the line of bone beneath the flesh of arm and hand.

Every detail was sharp and vivid, impossible to ignore.

She deliberately avoided meeting his eyes because she already knew what she would see there. Concern. For her, for his brother. And questions. A thousand questions, all for her.

The Pilenauans believed that someone who saved your life held it forever in their keeping. It was a common belief among primitive peoples, but tonight, right now, she found it oddly…comforting. It had been a long, long time since she'd been in anyone's keeping but her own.

But when Marx finally slipped out of the shelter, leaving her alone with Danny, Elizabeth couldn't help breathing a small sigh of relief. Danny, she could deal with. Derrick and her confusingly muddled feelings for him were another matter entirely.

Danny, however, brushed aside her offer of water and an MRE as well as her attempts to check his bandages and splint. The painkillers he'd swallowed were taking hold.

"I'm fine," he said blearily, waving her away. "All I want to do right now is sleep."

Which left her alone with Marx. Marx and the ghosts that whispered from the dark.

Elizabeth backed out of the shelter to find Marx setting up her own tent at the opposite end of the sandbar. If he'd tried to put any more distance between them, he'd have had to string it in a tree.

Yesterday, she'd have opted for the tree. Tonight…

Last night he'd slept beside her, solid and warm. Last night she'd felt…safe.

Instinctively, Elizabeth wrapped her arms around herself, remembering. She could almost *feel* him, feel his arm beneath her head, his breath against her neck, hot and gentle. She could feel his broad chest pressed against her shoulder blades, his belly against her back, his hips against hers, his long legs—

Despite her wet clothes, heat rose in her at the memory. She drew a shuddering breath, fighting for control.

After everything today that had been thrown at her, she realized suddenly, she didn't want to sleep alone tonight. God, please! She did *not* want to sleep alone tonight!

Tomorrow. Tomorrow she could be brave again. Tomorrow she could face the world all on her own. But for tonight, just for tonight…

She hesitated, then picked up a second MRE—impossible to tell what it was in the dark—and another bottle of water.

He was checking the anchoring stakes on her tent when she walked up.

"I brought dinner," she said. Was it just her imagination, or did her voice really sound that shaky? "Such as it is," she added, more firmly this time.

She tossed him one of the MREs, then warily settled

cross-legged on the sand with her back to the tent. When
he settled beside her, she nervously set the water bottles
on the ground between them. The move was instinctive.
In the dark he suddenly seemed so much...bigger.

Neither of them spoke. Marx made no move to open
his MRE, even though it would take at least ten minutes
for the chemical heating packs to warm the meal. After
a moment, Elizabeth tossed her own MRE aside and
promptly forgot it.

The night air was warm and humid, rich with the scents
of the river and the life around them. The jungle behind
them was silent, its secret night rustlings lost in the
murmur of the river. From the vantage of the shore, even
the river itself seemed tranquil, almost benign. For now.

At the thought, Elizabeth shivered.

"You okay?"

"Fine." Yet she wrapped her arms around her knees
and drew them tight against her chest. He was so close.
So *close.* All she had to do was scoot over a little. A very
little. All she had to do was *ask.*

Sitting down had been a mistake, Derrick realized.
He was so damned tired that part of him wanted nothing
more than to roll over and go to sleep on the spot.

Sitting down this close to Bradshaw had been a
mistake of an entirely different order, however. With her,
he had no interest in going to sleep at all.

He'd been shaking ever since she'd tumbled from that
riverbank. Not outwardly, but inside, where it was almost
impossible to control. Total terror could do that to you.

He was pretty sure his heart had stopped completely when she'd disappeared into the river and only stuttered on again when she'd popped back up an eternity later. By the time he'd finally dragged her into the boat, he'd survived a dozen eternities, all of them in hell.

Neither one of them had said a word about the incident since.

She hadn't so much as glanced at him since she'd tossed him that meal packet. He, on the other hand, had to fight to keep from staring. His hands balled into involuntary fists, only to discover that he still held that damned packet.

With a low growl of frustration, he tossed it aside, then got to his feet.

"It's late," he said, extending his hand to help her up. "We should get some sleep."

She shook her head a little, like a sleepwalker rousing from a dark dream.

"Come on, Bradshaw," he said gruffly, leaning down to help her up. "On your feet."

She came up heavily, not quick like she had at the top of that dead waterfall—was it really only yesterday?—but, like yesterday, once up, she refused to let go.

"Make love to me, Marx," she said fiercely.

"What?" The muscles of his throat squeezed so tight he could hardly breathe. He forced himself to swallow. "Now's not the time, Bradshaw."

"I know. But I want you to." It was a trick of starlight and shadow that she trembled. "I want *you*."

She swayed closer still.

"Do you want me?" she asked.

He groaned.

That was all the answer she needed. Without a word, she flung her arms around his neck. The move was clumsy, but somehow that made it even more erotic. She tilted her head up. He could see the tears welling in her eyes.

The tears were his undoing. He kissed her.

He meant to make it gentle. Reassuring, even. Somewhere in what little was left of his working brain he knew that's what he ought to do—make it gentle.

The trouble was, his brain and will were no longer in charge of his body. That first kiss was harder and more demanding than he'd intended.

To his amazement, he discovered a heat and a hunger in her as great as his own. As if she'd been waiting for that intimate brush of mouth against mouth, she opened to him. Her tongue flicked out to brush one corner of his mouth, then traced the inside edge of his lower lip to the opposite corner and back again. One hand pressed against his shoulder blade, holding her to him as if she feared he'd try to escape. The fingers of her other hand sifted through his hair and across the bare skin at his nape, sending chills down his spine. Her touch was teasingly light and incredibly erotic. Her breasts were crushed against his chest, her belly pressed flat against his, her center against his own hard ache.

Heat slammed through him. His breath caught somewhere between the going out and coming in, making a hard, hot knot deep in his throat. His brain stopped working. It didn't matter because instinct had already kicked in full force.

He brushed her tongue with his, swept the tip of his tongue along the sensitive roof of her mouth. He could feel the sudden kick as her own breathing caught. Her hands clenched behind him. Her nails scraped the bare skin at the back of his neck, making him shudder.

The taste and feel and heat of her rocked him. Instinctively, he shifted his feet, looking for stabler ground. Then he pulled her closer still in case she suddenly came to her senses and tried to get free. Thank God, she didn't try. He wasn't sure he could let her go if she had.

You ought to let her go, regardless.

Derrick groaned, trying to drown out that warning inner voice.

With an effort of will, he clamped his hands at her waist and tried to pull free. The little moan of protest she made sent his blood pressure soaring. He had to fight to get enough air to speak.

"Are you sure about this?"

There was a moment's hesitation, then, "Yes."

In the dark, she had become a silver-edged shadow. He couldn't tell if that breathless note in her voice was from uncertainty or a frustrated sexual hunger to match his own.

"I mean, *really* sure?" he insisted, a little desperately this time.

She drew back, pressing her hand against his chest and arching away from him. Starlight picked out the arch of her nose and chin, the dark well of her eyes, but left the rest in shadow.

"Shouldn't I be sure?" she asked. There was an edge to her voice he hadn't heard before.

"It's just— I don't want to take advantage—"

That's when she hit him.

He grunted and let go of her, as startled by the power behind the blow as the fury in it.

"Take *advantage* of me! You arrogant, pigheaded, puffed-up toad! Who do you think you are, anyway? And who made the first move here? It sure as hell wasn't you! If I needed a man to do my thinking for me I— I—"

She was spitting with fury and crying, all at the same time. When she hauled off to hit him again he had the good sense to dodge. The blow bounced off his shoulder. She rocked back, regained her balance and swung again.

"Oh, hell!" he said, and ducked, dragging her back into his arms.

This time he didn't hesitate. His mouth crushed down on hers. To hell with gentle. When the heel of her hand clocked the top of his ear, he grunted at the pain, then shifted his hold and kissed her again, harder this time. And this time, she relaxed into his embrace and kissed him back.

It was her fingers fumbling with the top button of his shirt that dragged his attention off her mouth and back to greater possibilities. Her knuckles bumped against his breastbone as she worked that button free.

Her fingers slid down to the second button. He loosened his hold enough to give her a little room for the operation and not a half inch more. She felt so good against him, so solid and right. He lowered his head again and claimed her mouth, careful not to interfere with the operation on his buttons. Her breathing was faster now, shallower.

His mouth slid over her jaw and down her throat. He could feel the pulse pounding beneath her skin, a trip-hammer *rat-a-tat* that almost kept pace with his own racing heart. Her skin was sweet and hot and slick with sweat.

At the fourth button her fingers brushed against the muscles at the top of his abdomen and sent fire shooting through him. With a groan, he pushed her away, raised his head, vaguely, disoriented.

"Your tent—" he said, and stopped. He couldn't think of what else he'd meant to say.

She took his hand and tugged him after her.

When she stopped at the front of her tent, he dragged her back against him and kissed her again. And then he set to work on her buttons.

The first one wasn't easy. The damn thing was too small, the buttonhole too tight. When it finally came loose, he gave a growl of triumph. One down, who knew how many more to go.

Two. Harder still. His fingers brushed soft cotton, then warm, moist skin that yielded to his touch. The second popped free at last. He took a deep breath and moved lower.

Three. He seemed to have grown extra fingers, and not one of them worked right. His breathing was coming fast and shallow now. It didn't help that she hadn't reached his zipper yet, that she was still struggling with the buttons on the waistband of his pants.

At four he gave up and dragged her shirttail free of her waistband, grabbed two fistfuls of shirt, and yanked. There was the sound of ripping fabric and the unmistakable ping of buttons flying off.

He reached for her bra. She brushed his hands away and unhooked it herself, quickly shedding both shirt and bra. Derrick cursed. He could hear the rasp of fabric, sense her motion, but he couldn't *see.* A hint of starlight outlining the curve of her shoulder and breast didn't come close to counting.

At least he could *feel.* His hands slid up her ribs to cup small, firm breasts. His thumbs flicked across the already pricked nipples. Her breath caught in her throat with a little choking sound. She leaned into him, into his touch, then wrapped her arms around his neck and drew his head down for another kiss.

The feel of her nipples brushing against the hair of his chest damn near stopped his brain entirely.

"I want you, Marx," she whispered against his lips. "Just for tonight."

Something in Derrick's brain shouted no, but he ignored it.

"Tonight," he said, "will be just fine." And then he started on the buttons of her pants. He'd manage his own damn zipper if he had to.

Chapter 12

It was the scrape of her bare skin against the wool blanket he'd left spread out on the floor of her tent that brought Elizabeth at least partway back to her senses. She flinched, startled by the unfamiliar sensation. These past few years, ever since her return to Pilenau, she'd always slept fully clothed. Now—

She gulped air and scooched farther back in the shelter. Marx was still crouched at the entrance, unlacing his boots. The thump the first one made as it hit the ground made her jump. One more boot, then his pants—

The sudden surge of heat made her head spin. Her fingertips tingled with the remembered feel of his skin and the springy curls on his chest. Her nipples ached, her stomach had gone hollow and the muscles of her belly seized even as they felt like they were melting.

It wasn't just the raw physical need rioting through her that made her dizzy, though. Last night she'd sat shivering in the dark with only her demons to keep her company. Then Derrick Marx had shown up, the absolute last thing she'd expected, and she'd awakened in his arms this morning to find that everything had changed. Since then she'd spun around in so many mental circles that she'd lost track of where she was, but every time she ended up back in Marx's arms, and every time, every single time, being in his arms had felt absolutely, undeniably, exquisitely right.

Which had to be all wrong because… Because…

Because why?

She blinked at the human shadow blocking the entrance. She was sure it had to be wrong, but right now, the reason eluded her.

There was a second thump, a scrape of gravel and *shoosh* of cloth collapsing in a heap; and then Marx was sliding into the tent beside her, and the stars reappeared in the opening.

Last night had been an awkward comedy. Tonight they fit together as smoothly as water sliding over polished rock. Her arms closed around him. His mouth claimed her breast. His hand brushed her hip, slid down across her belly, warm and rough, then lower still to the junction of her thighs. She sighed and rolled and opened to him. It was as easy as that.

His fingers found her. She gasped. Her spine arched and her muscles squeezed convulsively, trapping him inside her. He sucked in air—she could feel the rush of it across her now-damp breast—then gently nipped the flesh beneath the nipple, sending sparks shooting to her nerve endings.

"I want you," she said, thrusting into the cupped hollow of his hand. "I want you inside me. *Deep* inside me."

He raised his head from her breast. "Not yet." His voice sounded rough, his breathing ragged.

"Now." The determination in that single word startled even her. She'd never been so brash or demanding. So full of need. But here, with this man—

"Now," she repeated, and shoved.

She wasn't sure whether she rolled him, or he simply dragged her with him, but in one quick move he was flat on his back at the edge of the blanket and she was sprawled on top of him. For an instant surprise kept her poised, head up, hands braced on his shoulders, belly and hips pressed hard against his, her legs astraddle his. The side of the tent brushed against her shoulder and the top of her head, but she scarcely noticed. Myriad sensual details clamored for attention. Only one managed to get through the sensory confusion—the hard, demanding pressure of his erection against the inside of her thigh.

She felt as though she hung suspended from one of those distant stars. But then his hands were on her waist, lifting her, and she came back to earth with a trembling cry as he slid into her with one swift, strong thrust.

"Oh!" The word burst out from her throat. Her nails dug into his shoulders. She felt him flinch an instant before she heard his laugh.

It took a moment for her body to adjust, the strain quickly easing into pleasure, the pleasure swelling into hunger. She had almost forgotten how it was, how it could be.

He slid his hands up her ribs and over her breasts to

her shoulders, then back again. The calluses on his palms scraped her skin, rousing goose bumps of excitement. His hands slid down, over her hips, along her thighs and back to her waist. It wasn't a gentle caress but an erotic tug. Heat flared beneath his touch, then shot straight to her core. He paused, using his thumbs to massage the muscles of her belly. Then his hands slid down again, lower, fingers splayed, his thumbs still digging in to marvelous effect. When he touched her lightly, on that most secret, sensitive spot, she gasped and arched back and into him.

"Ready?" he asked.

She was already moving, lifting, sliding down, opening, squeezing, faster with each stroke. And those marvelous hands kept up with her, kneading, supporting, tormenting and thrilling her, all at the same time.

Dimly, as if from far away, she heard someone's ragged breathing, soft moans and quick gasps, but that was someone else, not her. She could feel the muscles in her thighs and buttocks stretch and flex as they lifted her up, then lowered her, then lifted her again, but that was distant, too. All the myriad sensations flooding her had sharpened, focused on that one key joining. Driven by instinct, she moved faster, harder, more urgently. And still he was there, deep inside her, anchoring her and urging her on.

Her climax came in a cresting wave, roaring over and through her until she thought she would drown in the flood of raw sensation. A cry of triumph ripped from her throat. It had been so long....

When she came dazedly back to an awareness of her surroundings, she was sprawled atop him, her head pillowed on his shoulder. His skin was warm against her cheek. She could feel the sweat trickling down her skin and pooling between their bodies, but she lacked the strength to move.

It took a moment more to realize that he was still hard and still deep inside her.

"Marx?" She started to raise her head, but he pressed her back against him.

"Wait," he said. "Don't move. Not yet."

Head still spinning, she obeyed. She felt drained and weak, yet exquisitely alive, all at the same time. She had almost forgotten what it was like to be this alive, this aware.

His breathing was leveling out. Each rise and fall of his chest beneath hers was strangely soothing, as intriguingly intimate as a kiss. When he rolled her onto her back, Elizabeth went with him willingly.

"Now," he whispered before he flicked his tongue in her ear, making her gasp with the unexpected spasm that rocked her.

This time it was he who set the pace…. Twice she thought herself on the verge of a second climax, and twice he drew her down, only to force her higher still, until even he couldn't hold back that exquisite, shattering crest. By the time his own climax had hit, she was limp and sated and…happy, she realized just before his final shuddering thrust dragged an ecstatic cry from his lips. When he groaned, then slowly, reluctantly, collapsed over her, she wrapped her arms even closer around him and, triumphant, drew him down against her.

Unlike the night before, they had no trouble settling together. Tonight, Elizabeth thought, the various parts just seemed to fit. Her head against his shoulder, his body pressed close against hers, his arm wrapped around her protectively.

Tonight, however, she could not sleep. The darkness seemed alive around them, the familiar sounds of Pilenau no more than a distant murmur compared to the soft in-out of his breathing.

When he called her name, softly, she wasn't sure at first that she'd really heard it.

"Bradshaw?" he said, then, more softly still, "Elizabeth?"

Strange, how good her name could sound when he spoke it in her ear. "Mmmm?" She couldn't quite bring herself to the effort of a full yes.

"That orchid you spotted, there on that bank tonight?" He hesitated. "You looked like you'd seen a ghost."

Her throat went suddenly tight and dry. She swallowed with difficulty. "I had," she admitted at last.

She'd never talked about her loss or her guilt. She'd never wanted to because she'd never found the words. But here, now, with a stranger who was no longer a stranger curled close against her, she discovered an aching need to tell him what she'd never told anyone else.

When she moved to sit up, he draped the blanket over her shoulders and settled beside her. Beyond the open flap of the tent she could see the river, black and silver in the moonlight, but inside all was safe, impersonal shadow. It was a good place for confessions.

His touch gave her courage.

"I had a daughter," she began, then stopped, suddenly disoriented. What came next?

I had a daughter. Four simple words that said everything and nothing at all. She'd swear she could hear the echo of them in the confines of the tent even though she knew that was impossible.

And yet…

I had a daughter. It was as simple as that.

Somehow, the rest of the words found her.

"I had a daughter," she said again, stronger this time. "Her name was Shanna."

Slowly, at first, then more quickly as the memories bubbled up, she told him about Shanna, about her short life.

He didn't interrupt, yet she knew he was listening to every single word she said, and every other one she didn't. It was enough, even for the hardest part of all.

"We'd had several days of heavy rains," she said. "When the sun finally peeked out for a while, we were both eager to get out. Our favorite place was a trail along a stream in the woods behind our home. She wasn't supposed to get near the stream itself unless I was holding her hand, but she spotted an orchid at the edge of the bank and—"

Elizabeth faltered. She remembered so clearly the look of delight on her daughter's face at the discovery. She remembered her own cry of warning.

She remembered the way she'd reached to grasp her daughter's hand and the way Shanna's fingers had brushed against hers just as the rain-soaked bank collapsed and sent its burden of mud and orchid and frightened child tumbling into the churning waters below.

The moment was indelibly engraved on her mind, every last detail, every scent and sound. She didn't remember much of what had followed—her own mad plunge into the stream after her daughter, the way the water had snatched her feet out from under her and sent her tumbling, slamming her against rocks, dunking her again and again until she'd been as blind and deaf and disoriented as she'd been in the river last night.

She didn't remember washing up on the bank nearly half a mile downstream or the hikers who'd found her and called for help. Nor did she remember very much about the hours and days that had followed.

She remembered the funeral, though, the dark scent of candles and the shiny oak coffin that had seemed so small under the mass of flowers. She remembered the cold look of loss and blame on Aaron's face as he'd sat there beside her, already gone from her, though it had been another three months before he actually moved out of the house they'd shared but somehow had never managed to make a home.

She didn't tell Marx all of it, of course. She didn't have to.

"And then Aaron filed for divorce and I came back to Pilenau," she said at last. The words had the feel of those old movies in which the last frames read "The End," just before everything faded to black.

"Why?" It was the first word he'd said since he'd asked her if she'd seen a ghost.

"Because I couldn't keep on at the university, pretending nothing had changed when *everything* had changed. Because this had been my home, once. Because…" She hesitated, then shrugged, resigned to the empty truth. "Because I didn't know what else to do."

She blinked. She was tired and it was late and even the river in front of her seemed fuzzy and out of focus.

Without a word, Marx leaned over to cup her face with his hand. His thumb brushed across her cheek, flicked back to brush her other cheek. That's when she realized her face was wet.

"How did you know I was crying?" She sniffed. "*I* didn't know I was crying!"

"The moonlight on your tears," he said softly. His hand still cradled her face, rough and warm and strong. He brushed away another tear.

The simple gesture was her undoing. The tears she'd fought against for five long years broke through in a flood of pain and grief.

When Derrick drew her into his arms, her last defense shattered. With an anguished cry, she collapsed against him.

All Derrick could do was hold on while sobs racked her slender body. He patted her shoulder, stroked her back, murmured futile words of comfort he knew she couldn't hear. He had never felt more helpless.

At least now he knew why she refused to leave Pilenau—cling to any refuge for too long and it becomes a prison that's virtually impossible to escape. And Bradshaw had been here a long, long time.

The torrent of her tears gradually shuddered to a stop. Derrick held on, waiting, wishing he wouldn't have to let her go.

At last she sniffed and shakily pushed away.

"Sorry. I didn't mean to cry all over you." Her voice was raw and slightly shaky. She swiped at her face, brushing away tears. "Thanks." That came out fainter, as if it had cost her an effort to say it.

"You're welcome." The night air felt colder without her close against him. He tried to think of something wise and comforting to say but came up blank. Not surprising. If he'd had the knack of wise and comforting, Danny would never have gotten into trouble in the first place.

And if Danny hadn't gotten into trouble, you'd never have landed in Bradshaw's camp.

He didn't much like the thought.

Strange. He'd only known her a few days, but already he found it impossible to imagine his life without her in it.

"You're cold," he said. "It's late. We need to sleep."

"Sleep." She said it as if it were an unfamiliar word, one whose sound she found intriguing. "You know, last night was the first good night's sleep I've had in a long, long time."

Me, too. He didn't say it.

It was easy settling into their spoon, her body curled close into his. It felt...right.

Derrick adjusted the single blanket they shared, tucking it in around her shoulder, keeping it away from her face. Her hair tickled his nose, and he smiled.

Her breathing slipped into the slow, steady rhythm of sleep. A minute later, sleep claimed him, as well.

A sound Elizabeth couldn't identify dragged her out of sleep. She lay there, sleepily conscious of an unfamiliar and, for the moment, unidentifiable feeling of contentment. She was vaguely aware of solid warmth against her back, of something encircling her shoulders and cupping her breast, and she instinctively snuggled closer into that protective embrace.

The sound came again, jarring her brain awake with a jolt that banished sleep and contentment both.

With a groan, Marx removed his hand from her breast and rolled away to fish the satellite phone out of his discarded clothes.

Elizabeth gave an echoing groan and hastily sat up to fumble for her own discarded garments. Despite the cover of the weak early-morning light that left everything shadowy and blurred, she deliberately kept her back to him. It didn't help.

In the close confines of the tent it was impossible to ignore the big and very naked man beside her, harder still to ignore her own nudity or her body's instinctive reaction to him.

Her nipples pricked into hard points. Her skin felt raw, as if he'd been interrupted in the act of making love to her. Muscles deep in her belly squeezed hard and hot.

In spite of herself, she turned to watch as he dug through the jumble of clothes and boots they'd left at the entrance to the tent. It was all she could do not to reach out and stroke that broad, bare back. She wanted so much to touch him, to pull him back to her. She wanted, suddenly, to know that she could fall asleep in his arms again tonight and wake again tomorrow, safe and warm and unafraid. She wanted to talk—just *talk*— and she wanted to laugh, just as she'd laughed yesterday afternoon, there by the river. She wanted—

Elizabeth drew in a sharp breath, stunned by how much she suddenly wanted, and even more stunned by how all of it was somehow bound up in this one man.

He gave her an apologetic grimace over his shoulder, then slid out of the tent. He wasn't even on his feet before she was forgotten. "Bear. Talk to me," he said, and walked away across the sand.

She ducked her head to watch him through the low opening of the tent. Such a beautiful body. Her own body ached, remembering.

Just for tonight, she'd said. She'd meant it, then. It didn't seem that simple, now.

A beautiful body, she thought again. And within that beautiful body, a good and decent man.

Cursing, she dropped the open tent flap and scrambled into her clothes.

When she emerged, she deliberately didn't look

toward where Marx, magnificently unconcerned with his nakedness, stood talking to his friend. Thank God he was a still a shadow among shadows. If the sun were any higher she'd be staring.

Head down, she crossed to Danny's shelter. He was still asleep. Even in the uncertain light she could see the lines of pain on his face. She knelt and gently felt his forehead, then his pulse. A fever, but not too high. Pulse a little weak and fast, but not enough to be really worrying. Food, sleep and hope, and not necessarily in that order, had helped him as much as the medicines they'd shoved down him.

It would take time for his body to heal, more time for his wounded soul to recover, but he would make it. She was sure of it. He had more courage than she'd ever had, and he had a big brother who would do everything in his power to help him, no matter what the cost.

She backed out of the shelter and went to check on the raft. It was something to do that kept her mind off the man at the other end of the little stretch of sand.

She checked the raft, the mooring rope, the river. She studied the sky. When she turned back, Marx was dressed, his phone nowhere in sight.

Elizabeth squared her shoulders, willed her stomach to stay calm and watched him come toward her. Even from twenty feet away she could feel his gaze on her like a caress, intense and intimate.

She wasn't sure whether she was more disappointed or relieved when, rather than kiss her, he ducked around her to peer into Danny's shelter.

"How is he?" he asked, keeping his voice low so as not to wake his brother.

She told him, then added, "He'll manage another day on that raft if he has to."

Marx straightened. "He won't have to." Taking her arm, he led her away from the shelter so they could talk without risk of waking his brother.

"Bear told me we're in the clear. The army's busy sorting through the Sword's camp. And their choppers…" He grinned suddenly. "They're so busy ferrying in all the bigwigs who want to have their picture taken on the spot that they haven't any resources left to chase stragglers like us."

She might have laughed if it weren't for the memory of bullets spraying across the rocks mere inches from her face and a white-hot beam of light sweeping across the river behind them, coming inexorably closer with every swing.

"There's even better news," Marx added, oblivious to her own hesitation. "Charley's already on his way. He's having to swing wide to avoid the army flight path, but he's coming. Another hour, maybe less. It won't be easy with all these trees in the way, but he can send down a litter and lift Danny up that way."

"An hour." Her stomach squeezed unpleasantly. "That's not much time."

It was plenty of time and she knew it. Plenty of time to wake Danny, eat something, pack up what little they had, maybe wash their faces and comb their hair. It wasn't nearly enough time for anything else, though.

Not for anything that really mattered. Not enough time to make love again. Not enough time to find the courage to say, "Take me with you," and be sure she meant it, whatever lay ahead.

"It's enough," he said. She couldn't tell what he was thinking. He glanced at the shelter where Danny lay. "The sooner I get him to a doctor, the happier I'll be."

"Of course," she said. Of course he was thinking of Danny. Of course he wanted to leave as quickly as possible. Of course he did. There was nothing to hold him in Pilenau. Absolutely nothing at all.

She forced herself to look away, then wished she hadn't. The two MREs she'd dug out for their meal last night lay where they'd left them, half-buried in the sand, forgotten in the urgency of other hungers. But that was last night. This was a new day, and Marx would be leaving soon.

"You wake your brother," she said, forcing a briskness she was far from feeling. "I'll fix us all something to eat."

She started to brush past him, but his hand on her arm stopped her. She looked up to find his gaze riveted to her face.

"Bradshaw," he said. *"Elizabeth."* His hold on her arm tightened. "Come with us. *Please.*"

"But…what would I do? Where would I go?" *Tell me,* she wanted to cry. *Tell me there's something there for* both *of us.*

She knew now she couldn't spend the rest of her life hiding in the jungles of Pilenau—Shanna deserved better than that, and so did she. Yet she couldn't bear the thought of finding herself alone in a world where she didn't belong.

"Go?" He frowned and let go of her arm. He didn't move an inch, yet somehow he seemed to pull away from her. "Come with me, Elizabeth. With us. You can stay at my place as long as you like. After that…" He stopped, as if he didn't care to put the next thought into words. "After that, when you're ready, you can go wherever you want. I won't stop you."

But would you want to stop me? Would you want to keep me?

She didn't say it. Just the fact that she *thought* it made her angry. The anger helped. Anger was always safer than fear.

"But…*where* would I go?" She regretted the words the instant she said them. Too late to call them back.

He frowned. "You can go anywhere you want. Surely you know that. With your reputation there must be a dozen universities and research centers that would want you. I know some folks…" His frown deepened.

She held her breath, waiting.

"If money's an issue…?"

It felt as if the sand had once again washed out from beneath her feet.

"I'm not worried about money," she said flatly. "It doesn't matter. I'm not leaving. I *can't*. Not today. I— I'm not ready. Not yet."

Soon, maybe. Maybe! But not today. And not with you.

Strange how…*hollow* that made her feel. She started to turn away, but he moved to block her.

She propped her fists on her hips, tilted her chin combatively, unwilling to let him see how much he'd hurt her. Unwilling to admit, even to herself, just how easily she could be hurt.

"In any case," she said, "it's none of your concern. And we've got better things to do than stand here talking." She couldn't quite bring herself to meet his gaze. The abandoned MREs caught her eye again. "Eat, for one," she added lightly. "I don't know about you, but I'm starving."

He hesitated but deliberately stepped back, away from her. It was only her imagination that the morning air had suddenly grown a whole lot chillier than before.

"I can definitely recommend the mac and cheese," he said, just as lightly. And then he ducked under the tarp protecting Danny, leaving her to retrieve the abandoned MREs alone.

In the end, she had the beef stew, though she couldn't have said what it tasted like. It was enough that it was hot and filling. She doubted either Marx or Danny paid much attention to their meals, either.

The three of them were sitting in a row staring out at the river with Danny sandwiched in the middle. Elizabeth didn't know if Marx had arranged it that way or if it just happened, but she was grateful for it. She needed as much distance from him as she could get.

They didn't talk, just ate and kept their ears cocked for the first hint of an approaching helicopter. At least Danny was too wrapped in his own pain to notice the electric tension arcing between her and his big brother.

"Take the rest of 'em," Marx said, tossing the remaining MRE packets to her. "I'm not going to need them."

With the dried fish and rice she carried, that meant she'd have more than enough food to get back to her camp without having to hunt for it along the way. She ought to be grateful, so why did the offer sting?

"Anything else I have that you want?"

Yes! "No. Thanks."

She looked around her. He'd taken down her tent, thank heavens. She wasn't sure she'd ever be able to sleep in it again. The few things he was taking with him were already in his pack, ready to go. Whatever he was leaving behind was in a small heap by the raft. "What about the raft?"

He didn't even glance at the thing. "Load it with whatever you don't want and set it loose. Nothing there can be traced to me. Maybe somebody downstream will grab it."

She didn't argue. There were a lot of poor people living along the banks of the Ipona who could use a raft, no matter how patched, and not one of them would ask any troubling questions about its provenance.

"You've got my address and phone number safe?"

Before she could stop herself, she raised her hand to the buttoned shirt pocket where she'd stashed the scrap of paper on which he'd jotted the information. "I've got it."

"You'll *use* it?" he insisted. The urgency in his voice made her ache. "If you need me, you'll call? Let me help?"

"Sure." She could tell by the way his lips thinned that he knew she was lying.

He hesitated, trapped, as she was, in that stilted awkwardness of long goodbyes. There was nothing left to say that could be said and too much empty silence that needed to be filled.

Where was that damned helicopter?

They'd already agreed, since they were on her side of the river, that it was better for her to return to her camp on her own. The risk of someone's spotting the helicopter anywhere near her camp and carrying the tale was simply too high.

Marx jumped to his feet, startling her from her thoughts.

"Might as well load that raft, then," he said briskly, like a man grateful for a distraction. *Any* distraction. "You can set it free as soon as we're gone."

And once she set it free, there'd be no trace left that he'd ever been here at all. Nothing except the MREs and one small scrap of paper in her pocket.

Danny was the first to hear the approaching helicopter. Five minutes later he was being pulled into the hovering chopper that had lowered a rescue litter for him.

Marx, feet braced against the backwash of the rotors, waited on the sand below. But he wasn't watching his brother. He was watching her.

Elizabeth had retreated to the side—to be out of the way, she'd told herself—and now maybe thirty feet of empty ground divided them. The roar of the rotors was almost deafening. If they wanted to say anything, they'd have to shout. But what was there left to say?

Wordlessly, he stretched out his hand to her.

Elizabeth wrapped her arms around herself, con-

scious of a sudden chill. She didn't move. Her heart was
pounding so hard it seemed to drown out every other
sound. Tears stung her eyes.

She could go back with him. Maybe she *should* go
back. Not for him or because of any danger he might
have dragged her into, but for herself. She'd watched her
father become so tangled in memories of the wife he'd
lost that he'd forgotten he even had a daughter. She'd
never forgotten she had a daughter, but she'd almost forgotten that she herself still had a life to live.

Where would I go? she'd asked Marx. *What would I
do?* They were the right questions, but she'd been asking
the wrong person.

They were questions she had to answer for herself.
Deluding herself into relying on him would simply
make the answers harder to find than they already were.

She raised her eyes to meet his questioning gaze.

Silently, she shook her head.

As if on cue, a cable and harness from the helicopter dropped into the air beside him. Without taking his
eyes off her, he grabbed the harness, holding it steady
against the rotors' turbulence.

She took a step back. Just one. He opened his
mouth, hesitated, then shut it in a hard, disapproving
line. Still with his eyes locked on her, he motioned to
be taken up.

His friends didn't waste any time. The chopper was
already rising, turning to move off, as they started to
reel him up. Her last glimpse of him, just before man
and machine disappeared over the treetops, was of

hands reaching to pull him in through the helicopter's open bay door.

And that left her on the sand, alone, the river on one side, the dense dark of the jungle on the other.

She let out a shuddering breath, then forced herself into motion. Pack first. She snatched it up without stopping. Raft next. Elizabeth tugged the tie rope free.

Marx had dragged the raft into the water so all it took was one hard shove with her foot to send the thing bobbing off. It spun once, twice, the freed rope drifting like a tail, the current catching it and sweeping it away. It was out of sight in less than a minute, but she remained standing there, blindly watching the spot where it had disappeared, until long after the sound of Marx's helicopter had faded into the distance.

Chapter 13

The streets of Pilenau's capital were as dirty, noisy and jammed with scooters, carts, cars and people as Derrick had remembered. Another time, he might have found the cheerful, busy crush entertaining. Right now all he wanted was to get out of the city and on the road.

He'd arranged to have a driver and Jeep meet him at the airport with any gear he'd need, including a rifle. He didn't expect to need the latter, but on Pilenau it was always better to be safe than sorry. Given the way the driver was bullying his way through the crowded streets, horn blaring, there was a good chance neither of them would survive the next ten minutes, yet Derrick had to force himself not to urge the man to drive faster still.

Five, almost six, days had passed since Bradshaw had called. It *had* to have been Bradshaw—he'd recognized the number his voice mail had picked up even though there'd been no message. He'd lost the first two days because he'd been in Cairo, working twenty-hour days and so busy dealing with the endless urgent calls from a panicked client that he hadn't bothered to pick up the messages on his home phone. He hadn't thought he needed to because he talked to Danny half a dozen times a day.

He wouldn't make that mistake again.

His attempts to return the call she'd made from what was evidently the village's only phone had failed. Either the lines were down, the static was so bad he couldn't make himself heard or no one answered. Voice mail, it seemed, wasn't an option in the Pilenau jungle.

Guilt, worry and hope drove him in equal measures. Guilt that he hadn't contacted her sooner, hadn't made sure she was all right. Worry that she was in trouble. Hope that she was calling to say she was coming back to the States as she'd promised.

He didn't dare let himself hope that it might be more than that, that she might be headed back to *him*. Seven weeks, seven crazy weeks, but she'd been in his thoughts every single minute of them. If he'd thought that he'd begin to forget her, he'd been wrong.

He didn't just think about her. He *missed* her. *Needed* her.

A sudden swerve threw him hard against the Jeep's door. The accompanying blare on the horn as the driver roared around an oxcart blocking the road would have wakened the dead.

Unfazed, the driver thrust his head and shoulders half out the window to shout insults at the offending cart rapidly disappearing behind them. Derrick sat up straighter and checked his seat belt. He didn't start breathing again until the driver, clearly cheered, had settled back in his seat just in time to avoid a scooter cab pulling out in front of them.

Seven weeks! Derrick swore silently. The first week, when Danny was in the hospital, and the press had driven them both crazy, had been hell. The next couple had been worse as Danny's elation at being rescued had given way to depression and endless self-recrimination.

Things had gotten better when a psychologist experienced with posttraumatic stress had started helping Danny cope with the memory of what he'd endured. At the psychologist's suggestion, Derrick had joined in family counseling, as well. It was one of the best decisions he'd ever made. It hadn't solved all their problems, but they were learning.

And, of course, there'd been his job. The Cairo trip had been his first since he'd brought Danny home, but he'd spent a lot of long hard hours in the office before that, trying to catch up. Thank God he had a boss who understood why he'd had to do what he did. Understanding hadn't, however, kept Gerritsen from submitting a mind-staggeringly big bill for services, as he'd dryly put it, rendered without benefit of prior approval.

At least one worry was gone—discreet inquiries with Pilenau government officials had confirmed that Danny had already been forgotten. They were too busy dealing with the members of the Sword now crowding the island's one small prison to waste time on one unimportant American who'd already left the country.

What kept Derrick awake at night was not the thought of the terrorists in the hands of Pilenau's government, but the thought of those still at large in Pilenau's jungles. That, and vivid memories of a woman he'd never thought to find. Just the thought of her was enough to make his heart rate soar.

He'd found himself with strange thoughts. Of marriage and kids and a minivan. At first, he'd thought it was a delusion brought on by exhaustion, stress and the unexpected intimacy with an extraordinarily beautiful woman, no matter how battered and dirty she'd been. He'd given in to the inevitable the day he'd found himself eyeing his kitchen and thinking maybe he ought to buy a bigger house, one with more bedrooms and bathrooms. One with a two-car garage for the minivan.

Night after night she'd stalked his dreams, tough, proud, vulnerable and infinitely desirable. He'd go to sleep thinking of her and wake up wanting her more than he'd ever wanted anything in his life. He found himself stopping on the street, his attention caught by a fleeting resemblance in a passerby, a way of walking, perhaps, or a casual lift of a shoulder, a mocking tilt to the head. The glimpses only made the distances that divided him from her that much harder to accept.

He'd started a hundred letters to her and had crumpled every one and tossed it aside, knowing there was nothing he could say that would make sense unless she was there to hear it.

Three days after he'd first come back to the States, he'd bought himself an open round-trip ticket to Pilenau and a second one-way ticket, Pilenau to home, in her name. He had told himself he would use the ticket next week, or maybe the next, as soon as he had a couple days free. It had taken him awhile to admit that he hadn't used the ticket because he was afraid he'd be coming home with that one-way still in his pocket.

But she *had* called, at last, and whatever she'd wanted to tell him had been something she couldn't leave on an answering machine.

Derrick grabbed the door as the vehicle swerved to miss a suicidal chicken bent on crossing the road. As he righted himself, he spotted the indignant bird in the side-view mirror, wings flapping wildly, squawking and scurrying for cover. He turned his gaze back to the road ahead and got a better grip on the door.

Finally, Derrick couldn't take it anymore. "Can't you go any faster?" he said.

The driver glanced at him, flashing a delighted grin. "Faster, mister? You bet!" he said, and happily ramped down on the accelerator.

It was the only public phone in the village. Actually, it was the only phone, period. It was black, heavy, awkward to hold, and it had an old-fashioned rotary dial that tended to stick every time you went past the four. For five years, other than for mail that could take weeks, even months, to arrive at its destination, the phone had been Elizabeth's only link with the outside world. She knew that the connection would be bad and that she would end up shouting if she wanted to make herself understood.

The problem wasn't the phone. The problem was that in a village like this, "public" meant *public*.

For as long as she could remember, the phone sat on the end of a massive, hand-sawn plank of teak almost twelve feet long that had served as the front counter of the village's only store. At the opposite end of the counter Mrs. Tran filled orders, took money and dispensed gossip with equal enthusiasm. No topic was too trivial to be above her notice, but phone conversations ranked higher than mere run-of-the-mill chats, and calls to faraway places like the United States ranked higher still. And whatever Mrs. Tran missed, the customers patiently waiting to place their orders would be sure to catch. By the time Elizabeth got back to her camp, half the village would know what she'd said.

While she listened to the clicks and beeps as the call made its connections, Elizabeth leaned against the counter, grateful for the dim light that hid her shaky hands.

The phone at the other end started ringing.

She casually turned her back on her audience, then propped the phone between shoulder and ear and wiped her sweating palms on the front of her shirt. She'd attempted this same call a week ago, but instead of leaving a message she'd just stood there, dry-mouthed, while the words jammed in her throat. When the distant voice mail system automatically cut her off she'd almost sobbed in relief.

If it hadn't been for Mama Bimani's confirming her own suspicions this morning, she wasn't sure she'd have worked up the courage to try a second time.

The distinctive beep as her call was transferred to voice mail made her shoulders sag.

"This is Marx. Leave a message."

To hell with the static on the line. The voice, so well-remembered, made her heart skip a beat, just as it had the first time she'd called.

"It's me, Marx. Bradshaw. I—" She hesitated. There were so many things she wanted to say, so much more she *needed* to say, and no time for any of it. "I'm coming back to the States. Some more packing then…"

Then…*what?* She still wasn't sure.

"I'll give you a call when I get there. We need—" She swallowed nervously. "We need to talk. I—"

Another beep cut her off abruptly.

Elizabeth snatched the phone from her ear. Damned machines! Damned, rude, impersonal machines!

She took a deep breath and very, very carefully, set the thing back in its cradle. It was that or slam it on the floor.

Her audience looked as disappointed as she felt.

"Not there," she said brightly, as if they hadn't already figured that out.

Mrs. Tran nodded sympathetically. "You wait, try again later, Dr. Lizzie, yes? This afternoon maybe?" Despite all the years she'd managed the phone, Mrs. Tran still had only a weak understanding of time differences. "Or maybe you write another letter?"

"Not today, Mrs. Tran," Elizabeth said, gathering up

the string bag containing her few purchases and the rifle she'd left propped against the counter. "I'm tired of writing letters."

With polite nods all around, she slipped out of the store. It had taken all her courage to make that call. The thought of putting everything she had to tell Marx in a letter was too overwhelming even to consider. Besides, she'd told Mrs. Tran the truth—she was tired of writing letters.

Over the past seven weeks she'd forced herself to write to every academic contact she could think of, letting them know she was planning to return to the States and that she needed a job. She'd told herself that leaving would be easier if she had something to go back for, but those letters had been far harder to write than she'd expected. Only the memory of her father, who'd rejected every teaching and research offer he'd ever received until finally the offers stopped coming at all, had kept her going.

Despite the vagaries of international mail, she'd already had three offers for temporary positions with possibilities for something more permanent in the future. They were excellent offers—good universities working with people she liked and admired—but not one of them appealed to her. She couldn't think of anything that did. Or rather, she couldn't think of any *academic* position that appealed.

What she wanted, what she dreamed of, was something she knew was beyond her reach.

If she'd thought, when she'd watched Marx's helicopter vanish in the distance, that she'd quickly get over him, she'd been wrong. He haunted her, waking and sleeping. She remembered so much she'd thought she'd forget—that rare, crooked smile of his, the way his brows knit when he was thinking hard, the feel of his hand on her skin, the warmth of his body pressed close against hers.

Thanks to his so rudely shaking her out of her self-pitying existence, she'd been forced to confront Shanna's death and come to terms with it at last. She would always mourn her daughter, but the bitter anguish of guilt and self-blame that had tormented her for so long was finally, slowly, beginning to fade.

In its place, however, had come a longing that devoured whatever solace she'd once found in her beloved orchids. Marx's intrusion into her rigidly circumscribed life had shaken loose feelings she'd thought long dead, needs she'd thought she'd put behind her—for love, for laughter, for shared intimacies and shared troubles, for the friendship and support of another human being who was truly part of her life, not just peripheral to it.

Which was insane. In the seven weeks since Marx had left Pilenau, she'd had no call from him, no letter. The man had turned her life topsy-turvy, then had forgotten she even existed.

What kind of a fool fell in love with a man who forgot she existed?

Me, she thought, instinctively pressing her hand against her belly, as if to protect the wondrous gift he'd left her. *The mother of his child.*

The miracle of it still had the power to shake her.

A baby. A future…somewhere. She wasn't sure where, only that it would be far from Pilenau. She couldn't hide in this jungle any longer. She didn't want to.

Elizabeth brushed aside a trailing liana, startling a bright green lizard into the bushes. She stooped to see if she could spot it, but it had already vanished.

She rather envied the thing. Two minutes from now it would have forgotten its fear. She, on the other hand, had kept on reliving hers until it had almost consumed her.

When she'd first suspected she was pregnant, her first reaction had been a bright and blinding joy. On the heels of joy, however, had come an equally blinding panic. What if she failed again as a mother? What if she couldn't keep this baby safe, just as she'd failed to keep Shanna safe?

For days she'd seesawed back and forth between heart-stopping elation and paralyzing fear. She'd think of Shanna's delight in the natural world—then she would remember that muddy riverbank. And then she'd think of Marx, wondering how to tell him, wondering what he'd say, and her thoughts would take another direction entirely.

It wasn't until eleven-year-old Niang had walked into her camp one afternoon, jaunty and happy despite all the perils that might have befallen him on the way, that she'd remembered what his father, Sahir, had said when he'd informed her the boy had learned his jungle lessons well enough to carry her mail on his own. She'd protested that Niang was too young, that there were too many dangers. Sahir had simply shaken his head.

"My Niang will be a strong, smart man," he'd said.

"But he must be a strong, smart boy first. How can he be strong if *I* do not believe he is?"

Elizabeth let the liana fall back into place. More than anything, she wanted her child to grow into a strong, smart, happy adult.

For her child's sake, hers and Derrick's, she would learn not to be afraid. No matter what lay ahead.

Hurrying now, she set off up the trail. Camp was close and there was a lot still to be done.

By breaking every speed limit along the way and having the good fortune to get stuck behind no fewer than two oxcarts, Derrick's driver got from Pilenau City to Bradshaw's village in a little over three hours. Derrick figured that had to be some kind of land speed record.

The hour's hike from the edge of the village to the camp, however, was beginning to seem twice as long. The closer he got to Bradshaw, the more impatient he became.

At least he was sure she was well and that she'd be in camp. He'd managed to learn that much in her village, though it hadn't been easy.

The proprietress of the village's only store had smiled and nodded and politely denied all knowledge of Bradshaw's whereabouts when he'd first asked. The local women gathered in the store had all been equally polite and equally uninformed until he'd produced the handful of kid-sized T-shirts he'd brought—for Niang, he'd assured them, at Dr. Bradshaw's specific request. That had finally broken through their protective reticence.

Yes, she'd been in the village just that morning.

She'd bought a canned ham, a half pound of sugar—or maybe it was a pound? The store's proprietress had authoritatively settled the debate in favor of a half pound—a half pound of coffee, a packet of dried chilies and a loaf of bread. She'd made a call to the United States of America, the second in a week, but she hadn't mailed any more letters. There'd been a lot of letters lately.

She'd also visited someone named Mama Bimani.

That last bit of news had clearly been of greater interest to his informants than everything else. He hadn't managed to find out why and hadn't wanted to waste time trying, but he'd been uncomfortably conscious of the women's smiling, avidly interested stares as he'd thanked them and made his escape. He hadn't gotten three feet out the door before a flurry of conversation in rapid-fire Pilenauan had broken out behind him.

The store's proprietress had promised that someone would immediately deliver those T-shirts to Niang's house. She'd make sure of it, she'd said. Derrick figured half the village would know about his visit by then.

Too bad he couldn't cover the distance to Bradshaw's camp that fast.

At least there was a good strong breeze this time. It made the heat a little more bearable. The path hadn't gotten any wider than the last time he'd seen it, however, and the damn vines hadn't gotten any less obstructive.

He swiped at a big one that was maliciously trying to tangle his feet, then wondered if it might be one of

Bradshaw's early warning traps. The thought made him grin.

But he didn't grin when he finally walked into her camp. He stopped dead and stared. There was something wrong here, but he couldn't put his finger on just what. The place was too...

A voice he hadn't heard in nearly seven weeks sliced through his thoughts.

"What the hell are *you* doing here?"

Heart kicking, he slowly turned around. "I was in the neighborhood and thought I'd drop by?"

She hadn't dropped out of a tree this time, but she still had her hair tied back in that damned ponytail. The clothes were just as ugly and practical, the boots just as clunky. And just like the first time, the rifle was pointed squarely at his middle.

This time, he figured he deserved it.

What, he wondered, would she do if he grabbed her and kissed her senseless?

Slowly, she lowered the rifle. "I called you this morning. I left a message."

"I got the first one."

She blinked. "I didn't leave any."

"I know. That's why I'm here."

She simply stared at him, eyes wide. The rifle slipped from her hands, forgotten.

"Bradshaw?" he said when she remained silent. How in hell could he have let seven weeks slip past without a word?

Two strides and he had her in his arms. He didn't get

a chance to kiss her. She thumped her fists on his chest and shoved him away.

"Why didn't you write, you jerk? Why didn't you call and leave a message? The villagers would have made sure I got it."

"I know. I—" He bit back the easy excuses that trembled on the tip of his tongue. They wouldn't have been the truth, anyway.

Yet how did he explain that he hadn't written because he hadn't known what he wanted? How could he admit that once he *did* know what he wanted, he'd been too afraid to put it into words?

Then again, he could simply skip the explanations.

"Marry me," he said.

That rocked her. "What?"

"Marry me. Please?"

He watched as his words filtered through to understanding. Watched as her eyes widened and the color drained from her face.

That hit him like a punch to the gut. He'd expected surprise, even anger. He hadn't expected fear. And yet… It didn't make sense. Elizabeth Bradshaw wasn't afraid of much, and she sure as hell wasn't afraid of him.

"Marry you?" It was barely a whisper.

"That's right. Marry me." Now probably wasn't the best time to mention the minivan.

"But…" She raised a shaky hand to cover her mouth.

"You don't have to say yes right away." Then, before he could stop himself, he added wryly, "Ten minutes from now will do just fine, too."

Her laugh was even shakier than her hand.

Derrick began to breathe again. He'd give her fifteen minutes, just to be generous.

She bent to pick up her rifle, carefully keeping her face averted. "Ten minutes, huh? Enough time for a pot of coffee, then."

He almost grinned with relief. A flat *no* wouldn't have taken ten seconds. "I brought you some of the real stuff. You can throw out that junk you bought in the village this morning."

That brought her head up. The wary look was back in her eyes. "How did you know I bought coffee?"

"I stopped in the village. In places like that, the general store is always the best source of information."

"And they told you? About me?"

"Only after I hauled out a dozen new T-shirts for Niang and convinced them that you'd asked me to bring them," he told her. "Before then, they didn't even want to admit they'd ever heard of you."

She let out a little sigh of relief. "That's all right, then. Though it was darned sneaky of you," she added over her shoulder as she headed to the kitchen tent and her coffeepot.

He ambled after her to dump his pack and retrieve the coffee. "I know. I'm rather proud of myself for thinking of it. One minute they wouldn't tell me squat, the next they were telling me you'd bought a canned ham and coffee and God knows what else. They said you'd called the States and that you'd been mailing a lot of letters lately."

He fished out the coffee, offered it to her, but when she reached to take it, he didn't let go. "Were the letters for me?"

Her gaze met his. She didn't blink. "No."

He let go of the coffee. Stupid to feel disappointed.

To his surprise, she didn't move away, just stood there, fiddling with the bag of coffee.

"Did they—" Her gaze dropped. "Did they say anything else?"

He frowned, trying to remember. This close, she was damnably distracting.

"They said you'd been to see someone called Mama Bimi. Bami. Something like that."

Her head snapped up. The color that had been seeping back into her face was gone again. "They told you about Mama Bimani?"

"They said you'd been to see her, that's all. Why? Who is Mama Bimani?"

She stared at him, white-faced, tense, nervously picking at the bag of coffee she still held until she tore a hole right through it. Ground coffee spilled out, scenting the air between them. She didn't even notice.

"Elizabeth?" he said softly, puzzled.

"You were serious? When you asked me to marry you, you really meant it?"

"I've never been more serious about anything in my life."

"How do you feel about…children?"

"Kids?" Now it was his turn to stare. "You mean *our* kids?"

She nodded mutely.

He grinned. "You know when I was sure I wanted to marry you?" She shook her head. His grin widened. "When I found myself thinking about trading in my Porsche for a couple of minivans."

When she still remained silent, he reached out and gently brushed back a lock of hair that had worked its way free of her ponytail. More than once over the past seven weeks he'd found himself remembering this simple gesture. He definitely preferred to actually *do* it.

"Bradshaw? Elizabeth?" he amended hastily. "Are you going to tell me who this Mama Bimani is that got your friends so worked up?"

He was suddenly pretty sure he already knew, but he'd rather hear it from her.

"She's the village midwife." It was barely a whisper. She'd shredded the bag of coffee so badly that all the contents had spilled into an untidy heap at her feet. She didn't seem to notice. "She says I'm going to have a baby, Marx. *Your* baby. A little girl. I'm not really sure it's going to be a girl, but…I'm definitely having a baby."

A baby. A girl. *His* baby. His and Bradshaw's.

He stared at her, the actual words so much more powerful than his assumption a minute ago. He was unable to breathe, incapable of speech or any thought beyond the fact that Bradshaw was pregnant with his child.

They were going to have a baby.

He felt like shouting for joy, but he *still* couldn't breathe.

A baby!

The thought that followed hit like a ton of bricks.

"You know," he faltered, suddenly not so sure of himself. "You don't *have* to marry me. Not because of the baby. If you'd rather— I'll take full financial responsibility. If you don't—"

He couldn't say it. *If you don't want to marry me.*

What if she *didn't* want him in her life?

Until this moment, he hadn't seriously considered that possibility. He didn't want to consider it now, but...he loved her. It was as simple and as staggeringly huge as that. And because he loved her, he had to be sure she knew that he wouldn't abandon her, no matter what her decision.

"Whatever you want, Elizabeth. I love you. I want to marry you. But if you don't want to marry me…"

The smile that lit her face was like the sun at dawn. Tentative at first, then rapidly growing bigger, bolder, brighter, until it made her whole being glow.

"I know what I want, Marx," she said. "I've known ever since that first night when you kept me safe from dreams. I just haven't had the courage to admit it. Until now."

This time it was her turn to reach out and press her palm against his cheek.

"I want someone to laugh with, Marx. In spite of everything, you made me laugh. I want someone to hold me when I cry. I still cry, you know. I still mourn my daughter and I always will. But…I want more than that. For her sake as well as mine. I want to learn to *live* again. Because of you, I know I can do that now. Alone, if I have to, but…"

She faltered, fighting against tears that glittered in her eyes.

"I honestly don't know what I want of all the years ahead except…I want *you*, Derrick. I want our baby. I want you to help me help her grow strong and brave and happy. I want—"

He didn't give her a chance to tell him what else she wanted. *He* wanted to kiss her. He wanted more than that, but a kiss would do to start. And she felt so *right* in his arms, as if she'd always belonged there and always would.

She opened to him willingly and he took everything she offered and more.

Touch. Taste. The burn of breath on skin.

The promise of so much that he couldn't even begin to imagine the possibilities.

It didn't matter, he thought, just before he couldn't think at all. In a world that offered him a life with a woman like this, every good thing was possible. Absolutely everything.

* * * * *

Enjoy a sneak preview of
MATCHMAKING WITH A MISSION
by B.J. Daniels,
part of the WHITEHORSE, MONTANA *miniseries.*
Available from Harlequin Intrigue
in April 2008.

Nate Dempsey has returned to Whitehorse to uncover the truth about his past…

Nate sensed someone watching the house and looked out in surprise to see a woman astride a paint horse just on the other side of the fence. He quickly stepped back from the filthy second-floor window, although he doubted she could have seen him. Only a little of the June sun pierced the dirty glass to glow on the dust-coated floor at his feet as he waited a few heartbeats before he looked out again.

The place was so isolated he hadn't expected to see another soul. Like the front yard, the dirt road was waist-high with weeds. When he'd broken the lock on the back door, he'd had to kick aside a pile of rotten leaves that had blown in from last fall.

As he sneaked a look, he saw that she was still there, staring at the house in a way that unnerved him. He shielded his eyes from the glare of the sun off the dirty window and studied her, taking in her head of long blond hair that feathered out in the breeze from under her Western straw hat.

She wore a tan canvas jacket, jeans and boots. But it was the way she sat astride the brown-and-white horse that nudged the memory.

He felt a chill as he realized he'd seen her before. In that very spot. She'd been just a kid then. A kid on a pretty paint horse. Not this one—the markings were different. Anyway, it couldn't have been the same horse, considering the last time he had seen her was more than twenty years ago. That horse would be dead by now.

His mind argued it probably wasn't even the same girl. But he knew better. It was the way she sat on the horse, so at home in a saddle and secure in her world on the other side of that fence.

To the boy he'd been, she and her horse had represented freedom, a freedom he'd known he would never have—even after he escaped this house.

Nate saw her shift in the saddle, and for a moment he feared she planned to dismount and come toward the house. With Ellis Harper in his grave, there would be little to keep her away.

To his relief, she reined her horse around and rode back the way she'd come.

As he watched her ride away, he thought about the way she'd stared at the house—today and years ago. While the smartest thing she could do was to stay clear of this house, he had a feeling she'd be back.

Finding out her name should prove easy, since he figured she must live close by. As for her interest in

Harper House… He would just have to make sure it didn't become a problem.

* * * * *

Be sure to look for
MATCHMAKING WITH A MISSION
and other suspenseful Harlequin Intrigue stories,
available in April
wherever books are sold.

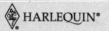

nocturne™

The Bloodrunners
trilogy continues with book #2.

The hunt meant more to Jeremy Burns than dominance—
it meant facing the woman he left behind. Once
Jillian Murphy had belonged to Jeremy, but now she was
the Spirit Walker to the Silvercrest wolves. It would take
more than the rights of nature for Jeremy to renew his
claim on her—and she would not go easily once he had.

LAST WOLF
HUNTING

by RHYANNON BYRD

Available in April wherever books are sold.

Be sure to watch out for the last book,
Last Wolf Watching, available in May.

SN61785

REQUEST YOUR FREE BOOKS!

2 FREE NOVELS PLUS 2 FREE GIFTS!

Silhouette® Romantic

SUSPENSE

Sparked by Danger, Fueled by Passion!

YES! Please send me 2 FREE Silhouette® Romantic Suspense novels and my 2 FREE gifts (gifts are worth about $10). After receiving them, if I don't wish to receive any more books, I can return the shipping statement marked "cancel." If I don't cancel, I will receive 4 brand-new novels every month and be billed just $4.24 per book in the U.S. or $4.99 per book in Canada, plus 25¢ shipping and handling per book plus applicable taxes, if any*. That's a savings of at least 15% off the cover price! I understand that accepting the 2 free books and gifts places me under no obligation to buy anything. I can always return a shipment and cancel at any time. Even if I never buy another book from Silhouette, the two free books and gifts are mine to keep forever.

240 SDN EEX6 340 SDN EEYJ

Name	(PLEASE PRINT)

Address	Apt. #

City	State/Prov.	Zip/Postal Code

Signature (if under 18, a parent or guardian must sign)

Mail to the **Silhouette Reader Service:**
IN U.S.A.: P.O. Box 1867, Buffalo, NY 14240-1867
IN CANADA: P.O. Box 609, Fort Erie, Ontario L2A 5X3

Not valid to current subscribers of Silhouette Romantic Suspense books.

Want to try two free books from another line?
Call 1-800-873-8635 or visit www.morefreebooks.com.

* Terms and prices subject to change without notice. N.Y. residents add applicable sales tax. Canadian residents will be charged applicable provincial taxes and GST. This offer is limited to one order per household. All orders subject to approval. Credit or debit balances in a customer's account(s) may be offset by any other outstanding balance owed by or to the customer. Please allow 4 to 6 weeks for delivery. Offer available while quantities last.

Your Privacy: Silhouette is committed to protecting your privacy. Our Privacy Policy is available online at www.eHarlequin.com or upon request from the Reader Service. From time to time we make our lists of customers available to reputable third parties who may have a product or service of interest to you. If you would prefer we not share your name and address, please check here. ☐

SRS08

Silhouette®
Romantic
SUSPENSE

COMING NEXT MONTH

#1507 DANGER SIGNALS—Kathleen Creighton
The Taken
Detective Wade Callahan is determined to discover the killer in a string of unsolved murders—without the help of his new partner. Tierney Doyle is used to being criticized for her supposed psychic abilities, but even the tough-as-nails—and drop-dead-gorgeous—detective can't deny what she has uncovered. And Tierney is slowly discovering that working so closely to Wade could be lethal.

#1508 A HERO TO COUNT ON—Linda Turner
Broken Arrow Ranch
Katherine Wyatt would never trust a man again, until she was forced to trust the sexy stranger at her family's ranch. Undercover investigator Hunter Sinclair wasn't looking to get romantically involved, especially with Katherine. But when she started dating a potential suspect, he had no choice but to let her in…and risk losing his heart.

#1509 THE DARK SIDE OF NIGHT—Cindy Dees
H.O.T. Watch
Fleeing for his life, secret agent Mitch Perovski is given permission to use the senator's boat as an oùt...but he didn't think he'd have the senator's daughter to accompany him. Kinsey Hollingsworth just wanted to escape the scandal she was mixed up in. Now she's thrown into a game of cat and mouse and her only chance for survival is Mitch. Can she withstand their burning attraction long enough to stay alive?

#1510 LETHAL ATTRACTION—Diana Duncan
Forever in a Day
When Sabrina Matthews is held at gunpoint, the last person she expects to save her life was SWAT pilot—and ex-crush—Grady O'Rourke. Grady is shocked when he receives a call informing him his next mission is to protect Sabrina. Though Grady is confident in his skills, she is the only woman who can get under his skin. He may be in greater danger of losing his heart than his life.

SRSCNM0308